HIDDEN
MOSAICS

HIDDEN MOSAICS

AN AEGEAN TALE

Alexander Billinis

ISBN: 1517287944
ISBN 13: 9781517287948
Library of Congress Control Number: 2015917692
CreateSpace Independent Publishing Platform
North Charleston, South Carolina

11-18-2015

To Phil,
With deep affection for the
man who is as a father to me!
With much love.

[signature]

To my lovely wife, Vilma Sari Billinis, who showed me the mosaic.

A thanks to several people is in order. To my children, John and Helena, as always my love and inspiration. To my distant cousin, Antonis Kourkoulis, who provided key insights hidden in plain sight; to my friend, my brother, Spyros Lagos, who suggested I travel to Izmir with him. These two individuals were instrumental in preparing me to write this book.

The wordsmithing efforts of Elizabeth Boleman-Herring and colleagues at <u>Weekly Hubris</u> merit a thanks, both for their editing and for their example.

Two other individuals, larger than life to me but departed this life, always need mentioning: my late father, John Alexander Billinis, and his late father, my grandfather, Alexandros Meimetis-Billinis. Without them, in every sense of the word, there would be no book.

As with my previous book, Milan "Jofke" Jovanovic of Sombor, Serbia, prepared the book cover and back.

Cover photo by Alexander Billinis, the view of Turkey from the Greek island of Rhodes, and back cover by Antonis Kourkoulis, view of Monemvasia, Greece.

Other Books by Alexander Billinis:

The Eagle has Two Faces: Journeys through Byzantine Europe

ABOUT THE AUTHOR

Alexander Billinis, a native of Salt Lake City, Utah, received his undergraduate degree from Georgetown University in 1991 and his law degree from American University in 1997. A United States and Greek national, from an early age he was interested in history, particularly the history of people rather than of peoples, and unofficial history rather than its official version. His love for history influenced his career, as he spent 15 years as an international banker, much of it in Europe of the financial crisis. His time in Europe allowed him to witness and to experience first-hand the mosaic of peoples and identities that is Europe, and this was indeed the subject of his first book, _The Eagle has Two Faces_. This is his first novel.

After nearly a decade in Europe, Billinis returned to the US in 2013, settling with his wife and two children in Chicago. In addition to work as a lawyer and real estate investor, he writes prolifically, for Greek, Serbian, North American, and Australian publications, and as a contributor to Weekly Hubris.com.

The Aegean, early 2010s. In the city of Izmir, known to Greeks, and to history, as Smyrna.

TABLE OF CONTENTS

CHAPTER 1

RANDOMNESS

Osman finally found parking. He parked his Golf deftly in a SMART-sized space, a two-step maneuver that practice had made utterly perfect. "Like a glove…" he said in American English, imitating Jim Carey's *Ace Ventura*, something that always annoyed Nilufer but kept the kids in stitches.

Locking the car with a beep, Osman headed for the café at the top of the *Asansor*[1]—his favorite view in Izmir—where all the tour guides just *had* to take their charges. Today's tour was no different—a big tour. Judging by their facial features and their alternately frowning and nostalgically smiling countenances, they were Greeks. Oh, how easily they annoyed him! Every time he ran into one of them in Izmir, there was an accusation on their faces, a sense of grievance. *No wonder my father hates them*, Osman thought, though in truth his father's anger seemed just a little too declarative.

It must be part of being a military man, particularly Turkish military. Turkish officers were a class all their own. They still lived with Cold War perks long vanished in the decaying armies of ex-Communist Europe or even the United States or Britain. Osman's father was a fighting colonel who cut his teeth in Cyprus in 1974 and served

---

1 Asansor: corruption of Ladino (the Spanish Jewish dialect used by Sephardic Jews) for "elevator." An elevator in Izmir that takes passengers from the lower ground near the port to the higher ground. Built more than a century ago by a Jewish Smyrna merchant to assist his elderly mother, the Asansor is now a prime tourist attraction.

during the decades of counterinsurgency against the Kurds, and his last posting was at the Aegean army headquarters. Well equipped with landing craft, this large force faced the numerous Greek islands that were sometimes a swim away. He had retired some years before, but he retained the bearing and being of a Turkish officer.

Osman's thoughts were interrupted when he saw his friend Cem, who had just finished his PhD work in the United States.

"Osman!" Cem yelled, and ran toward him.

But Cem stopped and hugged someone else, who good-naturedly but nervously pushed him away, saying, in English, "I'm sorry, but who are you? I don't understand Turkish."

Cem stopped, astonished, and with a look halfway between amused and insulted, said, "Is this some sort of a joke, Osman?"

But just then, the "real" Osman appeared, grabbing Cem in a broad embrace with two kisses on both cheeks. The "other" Osman stepped back a few steps, relieved that the encounter was a mistake but also quite intrigued. Cem looked at both of them, side by side, and said, in English, "Separated at birth?"

The two "Osmans" turned to each other and gasped. They had nearly the same face, thinning hair, and light eyes, and their olive complexions differed only due to the "other Osman's" clearly greater exposure to the sun.

"Unbelievable," Osman said in English.

"Yes, like a mirror," the foreigner said. Then with a slight flourish, he began, "I am from Neapolis in southern Greece. It is my first time to Smyrn—I mean, Izmir."

Cem saw that his friend was still in shock, and he said to the stranger, "Please, join us for a drink; this cannot be a coincidence."

Just as the Greek started to nod in agreement, the tour guide interrupted, in English: "Mr. Meimetis, you are holding up the tour, you know."

Harried and embarrassed, Mr. Meimetis embraced his twin on a whim and said, "Ioannis Meimetis, if you come to Neapolis, ask for me."

Osman barely focused during his reunion with Cem. After a quick drink at the Assensor as the sun receded, they were to have dinner in Bournova. He had forgotten where he parked his car and walked by it twice before Cem mentioned, "Hey, you said it was a blue Golf, right? Is this it, *budalla*?"[2] Then smiling, he said, "You really got shook up by this 'double' showing up. Maybe your father or mother got some, 'splaining to do,' as the Americans would say."

Osman ignored the good-natured rib. "Honestly, if he were from back home, or really anywhere here in Turkey, I might wonder the same thing. But a Greek?"

"Don't be such a narrow-minded fool," Cem countered as he slipped into the passenger seat. "What do you think has been going on across the Aegean for millennia, you idiot!" Pausing for effect, he then continued: "Now, if we can forget about your 'brother' for a moment, where are you taking me for dinner? And tell Nilufer that you won't be back before morning."

Around 3:00 a.m. Osman managed to pry himself away from Cem, who he dropped off at his parents' house, gunning for home through roads still laden with traffic. He opened the gate and parked his car in its designated space next to his father's old Mercedes, which was, as always, immaculately clean. His father's first-floor apartment had a light on. Seeing the car, the old man came out in a crisp robe.

"So, where were you?" he said in a demanding tone, holding a book half open.

"Why, are you going to tell on me to Nilufer?"

"I hardly have to do that; part of what you do in any organization is delegate. If there is punishment to be had, your direct commanding officer will do that!" he said with a wicked smile.

Osman started for the stairs.

"How is your friend, Cem, the Bayindirli boy?"

"Why ask where I was when you know, Colonel?" Osman said sarcastically.

---

2 *Budalla* is a Turkish word for "idiot" or "fool." It is also used in Greek, Serbian, and Bulgarian, and in other Balkan countries.

"I always like to know how my comrades' kids are doing. He is a smart one, but he spent a long time abroad; he needs to find a wife here and settle down. Turkey needs these brains to stay here rather than to go abroad."

Osman smiled. That was *Baba:*[3] always the Turkish patriot. He was sincere. Though Osman struggled with this mentality, it was somehow comforting and protective. The state built by Atatürk demanded loyalty and obedience, but it delivered on many of its material and spiritual promises. It provided Baba with a career and an education, without which he would have been a fisherman like his father, who died of skin cancer while Baba was in the military academy. While he lacked the almost corporate finesse of some of the highest officers—and their fluency in multiple languages—Colonel Omer Celik was nonetheless an educated man, and he owed that to the Turkish state and military, which, until recently, were almost synonymous.

From the staircase to his "floor," Osman looked down on the book. "Still pouring over history books, I see."

Baba looked down at his book: a memoir written by an officer from the Greek-Turkish War of 1919–1922. "You might read some of these yourself; you might feel more grateful and less smug. Too much English and that American literature."

"OK, Baba, I am tired and a little drunk. Whatever you say."

"Look, with your English and your master's degree in communications, you could have been a colonel at your age with diplomatic postings in your future. You had the talent and I the connections, and what do you do? You work for some textile company run by some fat bastard from Konya[4] who prays five times a day and pays his workers like crap, including you. His chief flunky calls you up day and night and interrupts dinner at my house—my house—on his so-called urgent business!"

Osman slowly found himself descending the stairs again.

---

3 *Baba* is Turkish for "dad" or "daddy." Also used in Greek and occasionally in Serbian.

4 Konya is a city in Central Turkey whose inhabitants are often quite devout Muslims.

"Come here, my son. Have a coffee with your old man, the dinosaur!" His father's embrace was just the thing he needed.

Sitting down, he watched his father's loving ritual of preparing Turkish coffee: the grounds, the water, the sugar, the small, cubed *loukoum* treat on the side. A glass of water.

"Here you go, my boy. I have not spoken this long to you for quite a while." In a voice halfway between hurt and commanding, he added, "Why is that?"

"Well, what with this job and the kids, when do I have time?"

"It's funny, I was at the front—at bases—but I always had time for you, your mother, and your sister. I was able to build this building so we could live together with each of us having our own floor and privacy, but also so we could be part of something bigger: a larger conversation, a larger family."

Osman smiled, thinking that somewhere another father and son were having this same chat.

"Maybe, Baba, our family is larger than we think it is."

Osman's confused yet slightly ironic expression bothered his father, but he pretended not to notice and said, "Well, sure, we are part of a community, a nation—we are Turks."

Osman took a sip of his Turkish coffee, then set it down, and said, "Baba, you know, in Greece, they call this Greek coffee."

"What of it?" Omer said, shrugging, "I think Bulgarians call it Bulgarian coffee, but it is Turkish coffee."

"But it looks and tastes the same, no?"

"Kid, what are you driving at? You have had this screwy look on you ever since you came in the door."

"I met Cem at the *Assensor*, and he greeted a man he thought was me, who was Greek."

"Well, we Turks were all over the Balkans; they all have Turkish blood," he said emphatically.

"Baba, he was the spitting image of me—as if he were my identical twin—and if I did not know you and mother better, I would swear we had a parent in common."

The colonel blushed slightly. "Well coincidences like that happen all the time. I think a lot of famous people used doubles, and probably everyone has a double. You literary types read too much into things."

"Baba, do we have any Greek blood?"

"Of course not; few Turks really do, you know. We are a unique nation, though we have brother Turkish nations in the East who…"

"…don't really look like us, now do they?"

The colonel rolled his eyes. "Nilufer is no doubt waiting for you." It was his ex-military way of saying, "dismissed."

CHAPTER 2

FLIGHT

SPRING 1821, ON THE OTHER SIDE OF THE AEGEAN

The small sloop with tattered sails had managed to evade the Hydriot and Samian ships giving chase, arriving on the Anatolian coast with crew and suffering human cargo intact, save for a few who expired, most likely from the traumas they saw.

Among the refugees was a youth in his early teens named Osman. His father threw him onto the Turkish ship—one of the few that managed to run the Hydriot blockade—as he was probably old enough to fend for himself. There was only room for him, and so Baba took his other two sons with him up to the fortress of Monemvasia, believing the rock to be impregnable, and in any case Osman's younger brothers were too young to survive without their father.

Osman had seen the Rock of Monemvasia every day of his life, for as long as he could remember. Only he saw it from above, looking down on it from his mountain village. It was a poor village with rocky soil, but it was nonetheless easy to defend against pirates, Venetians, or anyone else. Both Greeks and Turks lived in the village, but this did not make any sense, since everyone spoke Greek and both Greeks and Turks were related, because only in his grandfather's era had they converted to Islam. His own mother prayed to the *Panagia*.[5] She was a Christian, and there was no *hodja*[6] to tell her otherwise.

All that came crashing down that spring. The Greek Christians revolted in Kalamata and then the revolution spread everywhere. Muslims around them were its first victims. In their village, there was no massacre yet, but Baba, one of the most prominent men in the village, had gone down to Monemvasia with the boys at the first sign of trouble to get more news, and immediately the attacks began.

Osman had never been in a boat before, though he saw the sea from the mountains every day of his life. His small bag with a few coins fell out of his hands and sunk in the water below, "like it had been swallowed up," he said, to the needed laughter of the hapless refugees. The boat's horrible rocking made him sick, and he lost what little food he had, making his hunger even greater.

The ship was nearly captured by a Samian raider as it neared Asia Minor, but a Turkish frigate intervened and scattered the smaller Samian vessel. The trip across the Aegean had been harrowing, but short enough that the suffering was limited, save the inner trauma of families ripped apart by ethnic warfare, never to see one another again. It would be wrong to say families, as everyone on the ship had lost someone, and, in the way of refugees from time immemorial, surrogate families began to form.

The ship stopped in several places, and local Turks gave them food and water. Osman had no idea that the ship was going south and east toward Antalya, where the few refugees who had survived the massacres would be settled.

Antalya's port was a pleasant cove with crenellated fortresses; high, spindly minarets; and sandy coastline—all in the shadow of the massive Taurus Mountains, which kept the Mediterranean moisture on the coast. The craggy mountains reminded Osman of home, though the landscape here was more verdant and the mountains more massive.

---

5 Greek for Virgin Mary.
6 Turkish word for Islamic clergyman. Also used throughout the Balkans.

As the ship entered the stone harbor, all the signs of peace and commerce brought both comfort and sorrow to Osman. He remembered market days in Monemvasia or Neapolis on the other side of his native mountain, and now both ports were empty except for the Hydriots' patrols, and the Muslims there were no doubt decomposing in ravines.

The ship docked, and a mass of dirty refugees—more women and children—stumbled off onto the flagstones of the port. Local Muslims arranged for their care; the first trip was to the *hammam*,[7] which was separated by gender, and where the few grown men were waiting for the rest to steam and to scrub their bodies to a semblance of being clean.

The children were given clothes and bread dipped in oil, along with some fresh fruits. Osman had barely eaten in thirty-six hours, aside from *paximadia*[8] that nearly broke his teeth. The refugees found themselves among coreligionists who were generous and hospitable, but very few refugees could speak anything more than the most basic Turkish. The few members of their community who spoke Turkish were usually the leaders, and most of them never had a chance, as they were singled out for death from the start. In Antalya there were some Greek Christians, and ironically they helped the wary refugees with more complex linguistic needs.

Osman's temporary home was the courtyard of a mosque; his roof was a huge plane tree that was probably as old as the lovely structure itself. Osman's village had a very makeshift mosque, and he had once been to one in Monemvasia, for his circumcision ceremony. He remembered the pain of walking back up the mountains after the ceremony—so much that his father carried him most of the way. Crying out, he thought of his father, and of the great tenderness that that bull of a man had shown him. *When would he ever see his father again?*

---

7 Turkish public bath.

8 A very hard dried bread used by Greeks on long journeys, usually softened with water, wine, milk, or olive oil.

A month later, a ragged *caique*[9] arrived in the port from the *Mora*, and a local urchin ran to the mosque to tell the *Moraites*[10] about their countrymen's arrival. Swept up by a man from Falakro who knew his father, he and his fellow refugee ran down the flagstones to the port. It belonged to Yusuf Bey, a captain from Monemvasia. His arm was in a sling, but otherwise he looked fine and defiant. He disembarked to the embraces of the multitude, as he had been a fixture in the town, but when he saw the green-eyed Osman standing alone with tears streaming down his face, he ran to embrace him.

"Osman, my boy!"

"Yusuf Bey, where is Baba and Haris and Orhan? Did you bring them?"

Yusuf turned aside to hide his tears. "My dear son Osman, Baba Omer has asked me to look after you—to be your father," Yusuf said. Emerging from behind his cloak, a pretty blue-eyed girl looked up at him, "And look, I found you a sister! My daughter Fatima: she needs a big brother! What do you say?"

Osman took Fatima's hand. "You will stay on the ship tonight. Tomorrow we three will find a small place to live. We will fish here as I did there. You will be strong."

A new life began.

---

9 An Aegean boat used throughout the Aegean basin.

10 *Mora* is Turkish for the Greek Morea: the older name of the Peloponnesian peninsula in southern Greece. *Moraites* are from the Morea/*Mora*.

CHAPTER 3

FACEBOOKING

Osman sat with his laptop, toiling, as usual, long after coming home on some project his general manager threw at him. In his flawless English, Osman would create sales presentations and marketing copy for Hikmet, who would then present his own atrocious version of them at trade shows in Europe and America. Osman got to go with him once, and his fluent English and Izmir ease and sophistication won him points with clients, but not with Hikmet, who made sure that he would never travel again.

He shook his head at the memory. In a conference room full of company directors, Osman presented the extra orders he personally supervised, with e-mails confirming satisfaction with the orders and comments often full of praise for Osman. The boss barely spoke English and could certainly not read it, and he tossed aside these e-mails, saying with a sneer, "Hikmet tells me that you were more than friendly with a certain female buyer. He saw you at drinks and dinner and you failed to answer his call later that evening…"

The implication was clear. The boss, "Fat Husayn" was a devout Muslim from interior Turkey, and he insinuated that Osman had gotten drunk and cheated on his wife to get business. "But what do you expect from an *Izmiri?*[11]" the boss said, laughing. "You are merchants with no honor, just like Greeks." Osman might have added that a

---

11 A person from Izmir.

German customer had seen Hikmet leave one of Hamburg's seediest whorehouses that same evening, but he refused to stoop. As a result, Osman was essentially demoted and reduced to writing presentations rather than presenting them as well.

Deep down, he knew that the boss and Hikmet were trumped-up peasants from hardscrabble villages in Anatolia who had severe inferiority complexes vis-à-vis Izmiris or Istanbulus like himself.

"But they run the country now!" Osman's father often exclaimed, angry. They resented Osman's European look and manner, and his cosmopolitan, unveiled wife.

Another late night. Osman was finishing a presentation that, once again, he would not present: a well-worked, articulate, informative piece to be delivered by Hikmet in broken English that would draw sniggers from the crowd. Hikmet's secretary actually had to write out his English speeches phonetically.

Osman shook his head, both angry and almost sorry for Hikmet—and even his boss, Fat Husayn. The problem was that he suffered for it in terms of finances and periodic humiliations. But in today's Turkey, in spite of the headline growth rates, this was what was available.

E-mailed with attachment. Done. Now what?

The answer, of course, was obvious. Click over to Facebook—always on. Facebook was his constant companion—a reference point and an escape—but even this the boss had ruined. Though Osman had designed the company's Facebook page in Turkish and English, and had generated a lot of likes through his business contacts and his network of friends, his various postings in Turkish and English were taken, most likely by Hikmet, to the boss and portrayed in a negative light.

Looking over the latest garble on the home page, updates from friends in Turkey and abroad, his cursor moved to the search function. Recalling his "double," Osman wrote in his name as phonetically as possible in Latin characters. The name turned up a dozen matches, but trolling through the pictures, his "face" jumped out as if he were looking in the mirror. He clicked...

Ioannis (Yannis) Meimetis had few privacy restrictions. Personal information and pictures were publically accessible. Ioannis listed his relationship status as "It's Complicated," was forty years old, and lived in Neapolis, Greece. His picture—taken during the summer with a wet head, making his thinning hair shine—looked so much like a picture that Nilufer had taken of Osman in Urla last summer.

He quickly composed a message: "Hello Ioannis, my name is Osman Celik. We briefly met a few weeks ago in Izmir. My friend thought you were me. I thought we could become friends." He pressed the return key and sent the message. It was silly; it read like a wimpy attempt to be friends with another kid on the schoolyard. Osman looked at his profile picture—typical of a family man—with Nilufer and the two kids. To make his identity more obvious, he changed his profile picture to a headshot, which clearly showed his features so that Ioannis would remember who he was.

Just as he finished this, Nilufer got up and came into the salon. "The other person in our relationship is not even a person; it's that damn Facebook!" He looked up, suddenly. "Either get off it now or you can sleep on the balcony permanently!" Time to shut down.

He climbed into bed, but Nilufer did not want to know. She simply turned away and slept. Oh well, he understood. She did not like the idle gossip on Facebook and rarely used it, saying that it is no substitute for face-to-face communication. She spoke a little English and very good French, but had only traveled abroad briefly. She'd been to Greece several times and once to France and Germany. She had no network of friends abroad. A few distant cousins lived in Germany, but she found them either too German or too Turkish, and had no use for them. She was a woman who was devoted to her family, but one who valued her privacy and her alone time.

With no attention from Nilufer and hardly tired, Osman brooded, tossing a bit in bed, but not enough to wake his wife. He often had these midnight broods, usually about his career and his place in this world, but today, it was about this "double" of his. Why was this obsessing him? He knew full well that this was not his father's love child, and it was fully possible for people who were completely unrelated to resemble each other. Yet he felt that there was something here he needed to find out about.

And Greek, no less. He never really cared for Greece. As liberal and pro-Europe as he was, he did not like his nearest European neighbors, the Greeks and Bulgarians.

Yannis climbed out of bed, taking care not to wake Sia, sacked out in nature's own next to him. He had no interest in yet another round tonight. He walked into the other room, poured himself some water from the pitcher in the fridge, and grabbed a *koulouri*[12] that his aunt had made him. He remembered that he had left the laptop on because Sia had other plans.

He had met her last summer, in August, when she was in Elafonisos for holidays. The daughter of a laid-off Athenian CFO, she was used to the good life until about one year ago, when the Swedish firm her father worked for shut down its Greek operations.

Anyway, he opened the laptop, and instinctively his fingers typed "F-" and Facebook appeared: his account, not Sia's. He was looking for posts from his relatives in Australia or North America, but he noticed a red number one on the friend request prompt, as well as one in the messages.

Clicking to the friend request prompt, there was a name he had never heard—"Osman Celik"—with no mutual friends. His initial thought was to delete the request. He did not have his contact lenses on to focus on the picture, but when he switched to messages, he saw a note from Australia and another from this same Osman. Reading it, Yannis smiled. *Yes, my double from Smyrna! I had forgotten about that; I guess he remembered my name.* It was late, and Yannis's written English took more concentration than he had at the moment. Responding to Osman's sappy note, he wrote, "Glad to be your friend, Osman!" He

---

12 A Greek cookie of twisted dough, usually made around religious holidays.

then clicked back to the friend request prompt and chose "Accept." Sia started stirring; it was better to keep quiet to avoid another round with his ravenous girlfriend.

❧

Osman instinctively went to the computer, though he woke up late. He saw that Ioannis, or Yannis, had accepted the request, and he was overjoyed. He sat in the kitchen with an orange juice and poured through Yannis's photos, including some he took in Izmir. From these he deduced that Yannis had a girlfriend, another recent relationship, and a child who figured in most of his photos. The places in Greece where the photos were taken were unfamiliar to Osman; Greece, though nearby, was *terra incognita* to him.

Seeing him glued to the computer on a work and school day, Nilufer blew up, slamming the computer shut and startling both kids into dropping their juices. "*Budalla!* I told you to get off that damn Facebook. If I see it open again, I am leaving this house! You are one step away from losing your job in that fat Konya bastard's company; you had better focus or you can sit in a café all day with your stupid laptop, but without me and the kids!"

At work, there was a ban on using the computer for social media, which was deemed "damaging to our Islamic values" by company management. Freethinking types like Osman were the targets of the IT officer, who was also a devout Muslim. Osman tried to focus on work; he finished his presentations early and joylessly. Then he drifted out for a long lunch, which gave him time to think and to figure out what to do next. A long weekend was coming, and Nilufer had wanted to go to a school friend's beach house in Cesme, which was across from the Greek island of Chios and took several hours to drive to from Izmir.

"Do you mind going without me?" Osman asked. "I have, well, I just want to do some research alone this weekend." Nilufer sipped her tea; they had been married for eleven years, and she knew this brooding, bookish side of him.

"Yes, I think you need it. Good idea." She stirred a bit in her seat. "Osman, is there something going on? Is it just work, because God knows you are unhappy in work, but if it is something else, I ought to know. I need to know."

"A few weeks ago, Cem was here—remember when I went out with him for dinner?"

Nilufer nodded. "Yes, it's been since then. Is it because you envy his life in America?"

"My darling, I love you and the kids; you are my life!"

Cutting him off, Nilufer continued: "Osman, there is nothing wrong if you sometimes wonder about other paths in life. You are a thinker, a dreamer. I fell in love with that man, and I never thought you were not a good husband and father." She stopped for a second to let that sink in, and then continued: "Now, what happened with Cem?"

"With Cem, nothing; it was nice to see him, but when I was waiting for him, he thought he saw me and ended up greeting a man who looked like my double—from Greece." Nilufer nodded, less affected by that than Osman, who continued: "He was on one of those tour groups—you know, Greeks looking for their parents' or grandparents' roots—the mournful tours."

Here she nodded, and smiled in a mysterious, somewhat disturbing way, "Well, did you talk to the guy?"

"Yes. He only had a minute because the tour guide was shooing everyone into the elevator, but he embraced me like a brother would, and he told me his name and where he was from in Greece."

"Well, that was nice of him," Nilufer offered somewhat weakly.

"Yes. I felt a real bond with him, so I looked him up..."

"...on Facebook, of course!"

"Yes."

"Did you find him?"

"Yes, yesterday. I was a bit pushy in asking him questions, but I just think there is something behind this being identical twins."

Nilufer set down her tea, and moved closer to him. "Listen Osman, please do not read too much into this. I know that you are unhappy with your work. Your boss is a vile peasant—so much of Turkey today consists of people like him. You are looking for your place in this world, kind of like our country: not European, not Asian; Muslim, but not fundamentalist; democratic, but not civic. What are we? You are too smart to know that there are no easy answers. Your baba had the army and the 'father state,' kind of like the Soviet Union: sharp and crude, but it actually worked."

Osman just sat there, absolutely enthralled and amazed at the precision of Nilufer's feminine insight. She continued: "Now of course we are 'rich and growing' members of the G20, whatever that means—a key emerging market—but we have a prime minister who wants to use this wealth to turn back the clock and to tell Turks like me to wear a *feredje*[13] and not to have a glass of *raki* or wine when toasting our anniversary."

"I told Baba about it, and he just shrugged and said that because we controlled the Balkans for five hundred years, there was bound to be Turkish blood in the people there." Osman thought again for a minute. "Actually, no, he got mad. Like I was attacking his origins personally."

"That is just like my father-in-law, dear man! As if it is not the other way around and even more so! The Greeks were here, right where we stand, for thousands of years before our nomadic ancestors arrived," Nilufer said with an ironic smile. Then, frowning, she continued: "Do you know what happened when Kemal's troops arrived here? Your father's people are not Izmiris; most of mine are, and we know what happened. The memory and monuments of Greek Smyrna perished in the fire, which our history, of course, blames on the Greeks or Armenians."

---

13 Headscarf. The term is also used in Serbia and Bosnia.

"It is strange, but we have never talked much about this," Osman offered weakly.

"It was not a popular subject," Nilufer said. "In the days before the Islamic party, we were building the republic. We were all supposed to speak Turkish and to be proud of our Turkish blood and history, whatever that meant. Be loyal to Kemal's state and the military; be Muslim, but not too Muslim or Arab-like. Be more like, well, a Greek or a Bulgarian—just not Orthodox."

Osman thought about this for a minute, and nodded. Nilufer pointedly went on, "Of course, this hidden history was lost on you, an 'army brat,' as your Americans say. You were obsessed with America: its strength, its power, its freedom. It was OK in the Turkish Republic playbook to like America, our ally, but not to copy its society. Because you studied there for a couple of years and became engrossed with its literature, the idea of a more just and open society made it difficult for you to deal with our society, which is corrupt and not at all open. But the deep fissures in our own history and society, and the history with our neighbors, you never touched on," Nilufer said, with a surprising sense of finality and authority. "You do not want to know."

"Maybe that is why I bumped into this guy, my double, and I can't let it go," Osman offered.

"Probably, but I warn you: this fellow may not want a 'brother' or whatever. I don't think that Greeks are particularly open-minded about their history, either. The other thing is that this guy may just not be interested. There is a severe economic depression going on there."

"True..."

"But Osman, you are who you are, and you will not rest until you have exhausted this. Take the weekend off; just research. By the way, I'm sorry I was rude; I did not know about this."

CHAPTER 4

OSMAN'S "PROJECT," PART I

Osman kissed the kids as he fastened their seatbelts, and he kissed his dear Nilufer deeply and gently. Frankly, she still amazed him by how gently and quickly she cut through all of the stuff to the heart of the matter.

As he always did when his family was away for something, Osman felt an initial stab of loneliness that was quickly followed by an almost giddy sense of adventure. A stack of books in Turkish and English awaited him, as well as two open laptops, a large legal pad, and several pens in different colors. Here was his father's military sense of preparedness coming out. It was one of the few traits he shared with his father.

First of all, he researched Monemvasia, Greece's Rock of Gibraltar. A craggy outpost was joined to the mainland by a narrow causeway fortified by Byzantines, Venetians, Crusaders, and Turks. It had passed from Byzantine to Venetian and then to Turkish rule, and it was famous for its Malvasia wine. "I remember drinking this on that business trip to Croatia, and I loved it! So the roots are from there!" Osman said, pausing to think of the word "roots." He began reading again when his second computer pinged a reminder…

It was from Facebook: a quick note from…Yannis!

"Hi, Osman. I see you are online. How are you doing?"

"Yannis, good. Are you busy right now?"

"It is Saturday evening, my daughter is watching Disney, and my girlfriend is in Athens for the week, so I have a little free time."

"That's funny, my wife and son and daughter are away for the weekend, too. At a friend's house in Cesme, it is…"

Before Osman finished typing where Cesme was, Yannis typed, "…Across from Chios."

"You know Cesme?"

"Only through field glasses, but I swam quite near this and other coasts of yours. I served in our Special Forces from 1995 to 1997."

Osman paused. *How to deal with this one*, Osman thought. "Hey, can we do a video call?"

"Sure, easier for me. Writing English is hard for me."

Osman's shadowy image appeared. "Can you hear me?"

"Yes, Osman, and except for your accent, I think I am looking in the mirror."

"Yes, it is weird. I have to tell you, Yannis, that I think our looking alike is no accident, and neither is the fact that we met."

"Well, Osman, my parents never mentioned that I was a twin and that they lost my twin, so maybe it is just a crazy coincidence. After all, Greeks and Turks have been neighbors for centuries."

"Is your family from the Monemvasia area?"

"Yes, everyone."

"I mean, do you have Greek family from Turkey—the refugees from the war?"

"Nobody in my immediate family." Yannis sighed for a moment, getting a bit bored, perhaps, with the exchange. "So, Osman, what do you do for a living? Are you from Izmir?"

OK, he wants to move away from the personal. "I am the marketing manager for a Turkish textile firm that's headquartered here in Izmir."

"That is probably why your English is so good, not as mine."

"No your English is good, too. I studied American literature and spent some time in America: a year of college in New Hampshire and some time in Washington, DC."

"Wow, I have a relative near there, in Boston. We are all over the world: Australia, Canada, America—even in South America I have some relatives. People from this part of Greece went all over the world. If it were not for my daughter, I would be in Australia now, working for my uncle."

"Yes, America was great. I am so glad I got to go. My father arranged it," Osman said, and then wished he had not.

"How did he manage that?" Yannis asked predictably.

"Well, he was a colonel in the army."

"I see. Hey, Osman, you will have to excuse me; my daughter needs to go to bed. I only get to see her on weekends, and I want to read her a story. Nice talking to you." With one click, Yannis was gone.

Osman felt hurt—snubbed—almost like on the football field when he was not picked for a team early enough or, weirdly, when a girl rejected him. *Get over it!*

He went back to his sources. Both English and Turkish sources indicated that the outbreak of the Greek War of Independence in the Peloponnesian Peninsula, known then as the Morea or Mora in Turkish, resulted in the wholesale massacre of the Muslim population of Turks, according to Turkish literature.

The Greek revolutionaries rebelled against their lawful sovereign in 1821 and began a wholesale massacre of the Turkish settler population: civilians who had resided peacefully in the area for hundreds of years. By the end of 1821, nearly all of the Turks had been killed in an act of barbarism for which the *Rum*[14] Patriarch paid with his life in just retribution for the acts of the perfidious Greek rebels. Also, the Turkish population in several cities throughout the Empire, in justifiable rage, committed acts of retribution on Greeks.

14 *Rum* is Turkish for "Roman." Byzantium was the East Roman Empire, and the Turks still refer to Greeks in Turkey as Rums. Greeks also use the word *Romios* as shorthand for Greek.

Osman almost chuckled at the righteous indignation flowing from the Turkish patriot's pen. He did not doubt that the Greeks committed heinous acts because, hey, that's what an army does—particularly an irregular army.

One line, corroborated in an old history book he found in the British Library, gave him pause.

> Greek pirate ships prevented Turkish reinforcements from arriving by sea or ferrying the helpless population away from the burning Mora, but a few ships did manage to break the blockade and reach the coast of *Anadolu*,[15] where many founded a small refugee community in Antalya. They were known for years as *Moraites* (using Greek as a second language).

Osman good goose bumps, feeling like he opened a book in an old attic and found out some secret family history, like out of an English novel.

Just then, as if on cue, the key turned in his front door. Colonel Omer Celik walked in, unannounced, in his standard pressed shirt, jacket, and slacks.

"Hello Baba," Osman murmured.

"Son, Nulifer told me she went with the kids to Cesme, and that you were working on some research. I came by to keep you company. Is this for work?"

"No, Baba, it is for personal interest. History, actually..."

"Oh, well, my favorite subject—after soldiering, as you know," the colonel said, declarative as always.

"About the Greek Rebellion of 1821."

"Aha! Those Greeks: the cleverest of our former subjects. Theirs is a devious nation, and dangerous too. They managed to get the world to believe their myths and then set the world against us. No matter, they are in terminal decline, and we will grind them into powder, just as we did in Cyprus."

---

15 *Anadolu* (Anatolia) is the Asia Minor Peninsula.

"Apparently, they killed nearly all of the Muslim population in their southern peninsula called the Peloponnesus. Only a few escaped."

"Yes, they are very good at massacring civilians."

"Are we, Baba?"

"Take caution in the way you talk to me, Osman. I know that you are a global—what is the word—cosmopolitan type with little use for a fisherman's son from Antalya like your old man, but it was my hands and my gun that put food on your table, that sent you to your beloved New Hampshire and Washington, DC, and that built the roof you now have over your head."

"I am sorry, Baba, but you act as if we have never done such things. We have—the whole world says so."

"OK, yes, irregular forces full of bandits do terrible things in any country. But that is why a good, disciplined army is necessary. Well-led and well-trained armies don't commit atrocities; they fight and kill enemy armies."

"Baba, the German army in World War Two was probably the best trained in history. Are you saying that they did not commit atrocities?"

"Don't play with my words, boy!"

"Baba, what about in Cyprus? What did our army do there? You have never been that open about what you did there, except when you talk to others who were there—out of earshot of the rest of us, but not always."

"War is war, son! What do you know: a safe billet where you spend maybe one, two weeks at a time looking through field glasses at topless tourists across the straits near *Istankoy*?[16] Who got you that billet, boy?"

"I fear you 'protest too much,' as Shakespeare would say!"

"Smart college boy! Yes, throw in your faggot Shakespeare. Where are your good, decent Turkish authors?"

"Like Orhan Pamuk?"[17]

---

16 *Istankoy* is the Turkish name for the Greek island of Kos, one of the Greek islands closest to Turkey.

17 Pulitzer Prize-winning Turkish author, who often offends both Kemalist Turks and Islamists.

With this, the colonel turned, and walked out.

Good thing he already signed over the apartment to me, Osman thought.

Still, he felt badly about disrespecting his father. They were opposites in most things, but there was a great deal of love. The old man was a bit of a crab: hard on the outside, but soft and vulnerable on the inside, and almost wanting to shed the armor of his earlier years and his profession, but not knowing how.

A few minutes later, he received a text message. From Hikmet. Yuck. "Osman. Boss is coming in tomorrow. Wants to meet with you. Don't need to tell you to be on time. 09.00."

This could be it, Osman thought. He had spent most of his three years in the company butting heads with Hikmet, and he was clearly shy of the boss's approval. He also knew from numerous internal and external sources that Hikmet was out to get him. It may be just what would happen now. He wished he had not insulted his father, because he needed his old man's counsel and spine just now. Most importantly, he needed Nilufer badly.

Reaching for his cellphone, he called Nilufer, and she answered, "Hello darling, how is the quiet life?"

"Not so good—I got into a really bad fight with Baba. Over history..."

"Hmm, not so good. You know not to challenge him."

"It gets worse." He paused. "Hikmet sent a text. Fat Huseyn is in the office tomorrow; they want a chat."

"Ah, sorry darling. This is bad. This cannot be something positive; it is not an American movie, it is Turkish reality. I am afraid to tell you how much fun we had..."

"Actually, I need to hear it."

"We were out with Ilene and Suleiman and their kids for tea, and we met a friend of mine from grade school: a girl named Ebru Karamanoglu. She is easily one of the most interesting people from my childhood. Her mother is a Bosnian Muslim from Yugoslavia, and her dad is a second-generation Greek Muslim. She speaks excellent Bosnian and Greek. She worked for a Turkish company in Sarajevo and now works for a Turkish bank in Athens—I forget which one. I have her e-mail and phone number."

"Interesting."

"Yes, she and I talked about you—about your double your and interest in finding out more. She said she could dig up information from her circle in Athens: mostly academic, liberal types."

Osman warmed to the subject, glad to forget, at least momentarily, about his fight with his father and his likely dismissal from his job. "I would like to meet her."

"I bet you would. In fact, I could easily see you getting along very well if you were not married with children!" Nilufer said coyly.

"Maybe if I get fired, we can take a slow boat to Athens and crash at her place like we did that time at your cousin's in Düsseldorf." Osman laughed.

Nilufer joined in with her own nervous laugh, but she was serious when she said, "Listen: stand your ground. These guys are peasants, and thank God we have a roof over our heads, and we rent out my apartments. Don't let them humiliate you."

"Thanks, my rose. Love you. Kiss the kids!"

CHAPTER 5

AN OFFER YOU CAN'T REFUSE

T he next morning, Osman dressed in a sharp business suit, its elegance a sartorial riposte to Fat Huseyn and Hikmet, neither of whom could pull off such style. "Screw them. If I am going down, I am gonna look sharp!"

He gunned his wife's old Toyota Corolla to the office. Luckily, he had underground parking. The receptionist complimented his sharp looks. It was ten minutes to nine. He dropped off his briefcase at his office and walked to Huseyn's office. The door was closed, and the receptionist noted his presence with a smile. Hikmet joined him, giving Osman a smug stare, which he ignored, thumbing through an Izmir daily.

Normally Huseyn would like to keep people waiting—in his peasant mentality, such a petty humiliation made him feel superior—but today at 9:05 the secretary showed him in. "Celik, good morning. Fatme, please bring Osman Bey a tea." Hikmet looked up, momentarily startled, and tried to regain his composure.

"Osman, in two weeks there is a conference in Athens, the Southeast European Textile Association. We need to make a big impression there. We do not sell enough in the Balkan countries, where most textiles are Chinese on the low end or from elsewhere on the high end. Turkish textiles are familiar to Greeks, Bulgarians, and Serbs, and I really believe we could increase our market share. You would need to create presentations and first-class marketing materials; meet distributors and buyers."

"Yes, Husayn Bey, I understand."

"Hikmet could do this, but he needs to concentrate on Western Europe," Husayn offered, trying to soften the blow. Nodding to Hikmet, he said, "That will be all for now; I know you are busy."

Husayn just had to twist the knife. Well, at least it isn't me, Osman thought.

As the door closed, Husayn continued: "Now Osman, you have the right style for the Greeks. You are somehow—forgive me—like them. You speak good English; see if there are strategic partnerships or buyout opportunities. Greece is in trouble and maybe there are bargains. Take a week—ten days."

Wow, where did this come from? Why, I wanted to get to Greece, and now my job offers this on a silver platter! Allah is full of surprises and ironies! Returning to the conversation, Osman said, "Husayn Bey, it would be a great opportunity, and I thank you for this honor. May I add one request?"

No, Osman, don't blow it! Searching for the right words, he said, "Husayn Bey, in the past several months I have become more interested in our Ottoman past, particularly in Greece." Pausing to notice the effect on his boss, he continued: "I should like to take a few personal days to explore the country a bit."

Husayn was clearly moved, and because Osman's desire to go was obviously sincere, it warmed him the way nothing else could. "Osman, I am so happy to hear you say this. I had you painted as some Euro-cosmopolitan type without respect for the Prophet or our culture and traditions. You do the name Osman proud, one of our greatest Sultans!"

He sipped his tea, indicating that it was all right for Osman to drink his as well. "May your trip be filled with success! Do not concern yourself with economy. Make a good impression. You know how to do this with foreigners. Book a good hotel; make the right meetings. Explore the place; remember it was once ours, and perhaps Allah wills it to be ours again. Your father must be proud of you!"

How ironic, Osman thought.

After a few niceties, inquiries about family and kids, and pointed questions about work and particularly Hikmet, Osman left the boss's office. Husayn led him out and shook his hand, placing a card in it. "My personal mobile number. You call me if I am needed—anytime."

Osman tried to keep a poker face, which never worked. He saw Hikmet glaring at him from his office and fingered the evil-eye talisman on his keychain. "Garlic in your eyes!" he whispered.

Husayn sent one of the younger secretaries—a bright, multilingual girl named Hale—to work with Osman on logistics. "I will need your passport for a Schengen Visa and your itinerary, Osman Bey."

"Of course; can I bring these tomorrow? For now, book me a place at the conference and trade show. And call the printer; we will be doing special promotional material."

Osman pulled into his parking space at the apartment. Nilufer and the kids had returned early. *I guess she was worried about me.* The kids were at his aunt's house a couple of streets away to give Nilufer time to deal with Osman if what they feared occurred.

"Osman, my soul, are you OK?"

Having looked down, he looked at her with sparkling eyes and a smile. "If you had told me this would happen, never in a million years would I have believed it!"

The color rushed back into Nilufer's pretty face. "Oh thank Allah for this. So what, then, is 'this'?"

"Husayn brings me in—Hikmet is there too—and tells me that there is a textiles conference in Athens that I should go to, and that we need to develop the Balkan market. Hikmet was then basically dismissed, and we drank tea. I told him I wanted—actually, I asked permission—to stay a bit longer to study the Ottoman monuments and heritage in Greece!"

"No, you didn't!"

"Yes, and you know what? Old Husayn almost got tears in his eyes. I almost did, too. I meant it, and he knew I meant it!"

"Oh, Osman, this is great news! Good for your career and for your soul! You look younger; you look, actually, glowing. Like when we fell in love or when the kids were born."

That afternoon, no work was done, and the kids, luckily, remained with their aunt. After everyone went to bed, Osman got onto Facebook, clicked on Yannis Meimetis, and composed a message.

> Yannis, it is Osman here. I enjoyed talking to you briefly a few days ago. The weirdest thing happened at work today. My boss is sending me to a conference in Athens, and I am taking a few days to get to know Greece, particularly your part of the country. Can I take you up on your offer to let me visit you? Not to stay in your house, but perhaps you can recommend a hotel. I am very interested in learning about Greece; we are neighbors. I will be in Greece approximately from April 2 to April 17, and I have from the ninth to the seventeenth as basically open. Please let me know as soon as possible. Best regards, Osman.

His Blackberry beeped. "Probably Sia," Yannis said, rolling his eyes. He rarely got time with his cousin Panos, who was home for a few days.

He started reading and shook his head with a laugh. "No, it's my Turkish stalker!"

"Come again?" Panos said, his eyes narrowing.

"Oh, I didn't tell you. When I was in Smyrna a few weeks ago I ran into this guy—a Turkish guy—who looked exactly like me. Not like a brother, but an identical twin."

Panos's brows furrowed; then he broke into a smile. "Well, I always said you were an ugly fuck! I always thought that you probably had some Turkish blood from your other side!"

Yannis then countered, "Thank God there are pure sons of Leonidas like you, Pano!"

"What does he want?" Panos demanded.

"He is visiting Athens on business, and he would like to visit me here for a few days."

"Tell him to get fucked!" Panos suggested, but with more than just a bit of demand in his voice.

"Why should I? He seemed like a good sort of fellow: educated and what not," Yannis said defensively.

"Yanni, you know what happened to my father—your uncle—in Cyprus. He was gunned down after surrendering to those dogs—a true Special Forces hero! His name was on the plaque in *Megalo Peuko,*[18] where we both served. What kind of a sick fuck are you to invite one of those bastards into your home: the same lot who murdered your uncle?"

Yannis knew that Panos was not to be trifled with. In the Special Forces for more than a decade, he was also a *Krav Maga* champion, and the veins were protruding out of his reddening neck. *De-escalate! Let him say the next thing.*

Fists clenched, Panos caught his breath. "Yanni, you are my cousin, my blood, and I love you. You have been my family: your late father my father. You decide, but know that if the Turk crosses your threshold, I never will again. End of story!"

Guilt, blackmail, and threats, veiled and not-so-veiled. Families love to do this the world over, particularly Greek families. Well, Yannis had been bullied enough by family, and this ticked him off.

Walking home to his apartment, Yannis wished his parents were still alive to advise him and to mediate with Panos, whom he loved as much as his sister. He missed Sia, though their relationship still was too carnal-focused to deal with such subjects. Sia's sister in Athens just had a baby, and she extended her time there to help her—or perhaps she had second thoughts about the relationship? Whatever, he missed her now and wished she was near to comfort him.

---

18 Greek Special Forces training center, near the city of Megara.

Setting down his keys, he called Haralambos, who was probably his best friend in town. He owned a small hardware store, and he was probably in the back garden woodworking on some furniture—a side business.

"Hey, it's me, what are you doing, Haralambe?"

"Waiting for the Barbarians, what else?" Haralambos replied sarcastically.

How ironic that Haralambos would quote the famous Greek poem "Waiting for the Barbarians" at this particular moment.

"Me too. It's funny you should say that!"

"What did I say?"

"I'll explain. May I come over for a few minutes?"

"Suit yourself."

Walking, the trip would take ten minutes, but he jumped into his Jeep 4x4 and was there in less than two minutes, screeching to a halt out front and jumping over the side door.

"Shit, are the cops after you? Or me? The fiscal police would have a field day with me!"

"Um, no, it's me."

"Yanni, what's wrong with you?"

"I need your advice."

"Sit down." Haralambos turned off the saw, removed his gloves, and pulled up his own chair. "The doctor is in. Do you need a couch, or will my humble office suffice?"

"I had a fight with Panos."

"Your cousin? Obviously it was not a physical fight, because I would be talking to you in the clinic or through a bed sheet at the morgue!"

Nodding slightly, though annoyed at the comment, Yannis said, "The funny thing is that it is about something so random."

"What?"

"Remember when I told you that I met a Turk in Smyrna that looked exactly like me?"

"Yes, so?"

"Well, offhandedly I invited this guy to visit me here if he ever made it over to Greece. You know, the kind of thing you say just to be nice."

Haralambos nodded, pretending to take psychiatrist's notes.

"Well, he found me on Facebook. He called me on Skype. He was very friendly, but also very inquisitive. He tried to see if we have some sort of ancestry in common."

"Well, it seems a little creepy, but maybe not." Stopping for a minute, he said, "As for Panos, well I can guess the thought of a Turk—any Turk—sends him over the edge. Why on earth did you tell him?"

"Because I just got the message, and I innocently told him. I didn't think I had to censor myself with my cousin!"

"Well, it looks as if you did have to! I like Panos, but it is your business if you want to let this freak visit you."

"Why do you have to call him that?"

"Look Yanni, your life is complicated enough. You are divorced with a child to raise and a new girlfriend. We are in a Great Depression, and your work is irregular. This is not a worldly city like Athens or Thessaloniki. Not so much here, but in other towns the Golden Dawn[19] group is growing in strength. Your cousin, by the way, while not a member, is certainly a sympathizer. And many of his army buddies are open supporters. You know that!"

"Good point, I guess."

"So, if somebody here shows up who is the spitting image of you and turns out to be a Turk, it is going to raise eyebrows. Further, if your cousin makes his opposition clear to others, as a local heavy and the son of a martyred Greek hero, you are going to have some explaining to do."

"So, it's give in, once again."

"It's pick your battles, I would not fight this one, and unfortunately it may be a battle."

---

19 Golden Dawn is a fascist political party in Greece.

CHAPTER 6

OSMAN'S "PROJECT," PART II

Back in Izmir, Osman was busy preparing materials for his trip, but his eye constantly veered toward his computer and smartphone. "Will Yannis respond?" he wondered. It had been two days, and he was scheduled to leave for Athens in five.

At home and at work, Osman was stressed and irritable. Husayn was in Konya, but Hikmet noticed Osman's distraction and was certain to report on it. At home, too, Nilufer had become tired of his snappiness. "Maybe this Yannis guy just wants to be left alone. It is his right; he may think you are some kind of nut. Not everyone is interested in history. He may not like Turks; we did quite a few things to them."

Just then, there was a beep on his phone, indicating a message. As he reached for it, Nilufer said, "Don't even think about it when I'm talking to you!"

Throwing up her hands in surrender, she said, "Osman, my soul, get with it! I have arranged for you to meet my friend Ebru in Athens; she works for the firm's bank anyway, so you can connect it with your trip. She is very knowledgeable about Greece, and her boyfriend is a Greek historian or artist or something. They will take you to dinner when it is convenient, along with some of their friends. You will probably get further with them than with your Greek 'twin.'"

Again, Nilufer was wise and caring. He took her in his arms. "Thank you, my soul!"

Nilufer lingered, a slight ironic smile on her lips. Then, she was off to tend to the kids.

Tentatively, Osman walked over to the laptop, and a message on Facebook waited for him.

> Osman, I have received your message, and I would be very happy to see you in our town when you are visiting Greece. Let me know your schedule.

After that, all Osman's preparations went smoothly, and from irritable he became pleasant with everyone, including Hikmet. His rival thought it was because Osman wanted to rub it in that he was going on a business trip, which was normally the duty of Hikmet.

He prepared his notes and presentations, and steeled himself for several days of networking, though his thoughts were far from the business. He was, however, well aware that he needed this job, and that, as fate would have it, his star was on the rise. While he looked at Husayn as a peasant whose politics he despised, he also realized that, finally, he and Husayn had goals in common. Husayn was clever enough to let Osman run with the Balkans, because he knew that Hikmet was, ultimately, just a useful crony. As much as Husayn owed his rise to political cronyism associated with the Islamists, his ultimate success and sustainability depended on entering diverse markets and leveraging people with global skills. Osman had a great opportunity to define himself in the company.

The question is: would he take it? This also weighed on Nilufer's mind. Her husband was a complicated guy. Like so many men in their later thirties and early forties, he actively questioned how well he had progressed with his life. As a couple and a family they were at least as happy and harmonious as the next family, but Osman struggled with demons: career ones, identity ones, and a strange, gnawing guilt not his own.

Osman's late mother, Zeynep, had been a quiet lady from a poor Turkish family with deep roots in Izmir. Her parents and grandparents had worked for the Greek, Jewish, Armenian, or foreign commercial houses in then-Smyrna. When the Turkish army evicted the Greek occupation forces from the city in 1922, her family rejoiced, sensing that the infidels who exploited Turkey had been exploiting them. The port essentially went dead, commerce never returned, and from meager yet steady wages, her family sank into deep poverty. Zeynep's father, Mehmet, used to say, "Our republic is one of poverty." He taught himself French while working in an Armenian import-export agency, and he read any French book—particularly about labor and economics—that he could find. He married late—he was nearly fifty—to a young Izmir woman, and they had two children who survived into adulthood. Their son, Orhan, moved to Germany in the late 1960s and never looked back; and their lovely green-eyed daughter, Zeynep, studied French in high school and charmed all the boys of the neighborhood.

It was Orhan's trickle of resources that kept the family afloat and paid for Zeynep's school fees. When a young officer called on Mehmet to ask for Zeynep's hand, he could hardly say no. He found the officer arrogant and crude: a burly fisherman's son from Antalya who was as strong as an ox and clearly capable of great cruelty. Mehmet was poor and was known as something of a radical—hardly great for his daughter's prospects. With these thoughts in mind, he gave his blessing.

All things being equal, the marriage worked. There was a clear attraction between the green-eyed couple, and the violence that was part of the officer's job ended at the door to his home. Omer was a model husband, at least by the most liberal standards of the secularist Turks. Two children arrived: the first was Osman, who was named after the officer's grandfather in Antalya, and a daughter thereafter. Zeynep died in her sixties several years ago.

Nilufer reflected on her own family. That was complicated, but in Turkey such complications were best left to kitchen talk. She was grateful that her husband was a learned, liberal fellow whom she could talk to, though on the subject of her family she still talked as little as possible. Her parents died relatively early, and Osman only got to know her father. Anyway, back to the daily grind...

Driving Osman to the airport, Nilufer thought about their family history and how this, somehow, was a journey into that history. Her husband was fidgety and nervous, which was typical of him before a trip, but she sensed that it was something more. Normally it would be career nerves—worrying about doing well and navigating all of the difficult politics and minefields in his job—but this time it was different. She sensed that the trip would change his life.

Dropping him at the entrance with his luggage, she kissed him fervently. "My soul, be safe, be happy, be mine!" He slowly pulled away.

"Do you want me to come in?"

"No, it's OK. I am alone with my thoughts now."

"Remember, Ebru will find you at the conference and arrange dinner with her friends after you finish your work stuff."

Izmir's spanking new airport was not particularly busy this early Tuesday morning. The tour bus that lined up behind Osman was full of Greeks who were loud and speaking various degrees of English to the Turkish tour guides about luggage, gifts, and carry-on restrictions. They reminded him of the group Yannis had been in. In spite of the crisis, Greek tours to Izmir were booked solid.

Entering the plane, he found that he was seated next to a pleasant-looking younger fellow: probably Greek, but somehow different. "Excuse me," Osman said in English. "I believe I am next to you."

"Sure thing," the fellow said in American English with a slight Yankee accent.

Sitting down, Osman said, "Are you American?"

"Greek American, actually, from Boston."

"Ah, I know Boston. I studied in New Hampshire," Osman said, smiling at the memory. "How did you enjoy Turkey?"

"I was with that tour," he said, pointing backward and rolling his eyes, "until I took off on my own."

"I can imagine that was better. Where did you go?"

"Aydin."

"Really. That's sort of off the tourist path. Why there?"

"My great grandmother—she was born there."

After an awkward pause, Osman cleared his throat. The fellow broke in, offering his hand. "My name is Peter, by the way. Peter Sarafoglou."

"Osman Celik, nice to meet you." Fidgeting a bit, he continued. "Did you, um, enjoy Aydin?"

"It was easily the most incredible experience I ever had," Peter said, his eyes sparkling.

Osman smiled, and Peter went on: "Well, I ditched this Greek tour on the second day. We had just been to Urla, and I wanted to get away from these people and to spend some quality time in Aydin. At the hotel they hooked me up with the bus station, and off I went the next morning. I got into Aydin early afternoon and found a tavern to eat at. They could not speak English, but they called a guy from a nearby shop who could. He sat down for a few minutes, and I told him why I was here. Then he looked at me for a minute, punched something in his cell phone, and ten minutes later, his father arrived, smiling, and in very bad English welcomed me to Aydin and offered me a place to stay in their house. 'My wife will cook a good local type food,' he said, 'and my house is your house.'"

"Quite a story," Osman said, then tentatively he said, "I am going to Greece on business, but I plan to stay a bit longer to find, I think, my own roots."

"That's it!" Peter exclaimed. "Roots is right. I felt more of a connection in Aydin than anywhere in Greece or America. It astounded me."

Osman was ready to say something, but Peter continued, tearing up slightly. "You know, my great grandmother asked me to bring back some earth, some dirt, from Aydin. When Baba Turgut, the head of the house, heard this, he went and bought a cedar box with a scene of the city to put the earth in."

Here, Osman's tears began to flow. "These personal histories are so different from, well, history."

"You can say that again! The last day I am there, the family brings over an old, old man—a relic at ninety-eight years old—named Yusuf Effendi. I kissed his hand, and he told me about Aydin in the days before the exchange, when Greeks and Turks played together as children, did business together, respected one another's holidays and customs."

"Well, then why do these stories all end the same way?" Osman said, as if he were talking to himself.

"The old man commented on that, too. He said, 'Allah wants all His children in the garden, but some men, including those that speak for Allah, want to divide the garden and kick others out.' War comes in, makes you take sides. He blamed the Greeks for the expulsion, but then said, 'Our republic lost its right hand, and the right part of its heart and soul, when the Christians were expelled. For me, there will always be this wound,' he said, rubbing his heart."

The conversation took most of the forty-five minute trip across the Aegean; they were descending into Athens. Absorbed in the conversation, Osman had no chance to look out the window. The plane was flying low as it approached Athens, where smog was visible in the distance. The villas, farms, and houses of semirural, semisuburban Attica shone in the late winter sun. Landing softly, as the plane taxied to its spot, Peter said, "Welcome to Greece. I hope you find what you seek here!"

"I just checked my messages. I have a meeting at 3:00 p.m. in my hotel lobby with a Greek distributor. Otherwise, I wanted to buy you Athens's best lunch."

"I am getting Athens's best lunch at my aunt's house in Nea Ionia, and I wanted to invite you. It is very much cuisine from Aydin; you would recognize it!"

The sadness on Osman's face was obvious. "That would have been wonderful. Damned job!"

"Don't worry Osman, I will come back to Turkey, and you can host me in Izmir!" Peter said, laughingly. "How 'bout it?"

"It's a deal; I will hold you to it!" Osman said, handing out a card to Peter. My personal e-mail, mobile, and address are on the back of the card.

After passport control and customs, they said goodbye, shook hands, and then Peter tentatively hugged him. "I just know this trip will be to you what my trip to Turkey was to me!"

With that, he was off.

CHAPTER 7

ATHENS

Osman asked a policeman for a taxi stand. He wordlessly and rudely jerked his head to one side. Sliding into the first cab at the front of a long line, the cabbie, looking at Osman's features, said in Greek, "*Pou pame, Kyrie?*"

"I am going to the Athens Hilton on Vasilissis Sofias Avenue."

"And I am a cab driver. Do you think I don't know where it is?" The driver's English was well-learned, just out of practice. "Sorry, just a joke. Where you from: Italy? Bulgaria?"

"No. Turkey."

"Aha! My parents were from Constantinople—your Istanbul." Then he switched to an unsteady Turkish. "They used to speak Turkish when they did not want us kids to understand, so of course, we learned Turkish!"

"When did they, um, leave?"

"They were deported in 1964. I was born about nine months later, here in Athens. They joked later on that, on one of their last nights there, they had a great night on the town, went to all of their favorite spots, and spent money like water, because they could not take it with them. Little did they know they got a souvenir: me," the cabbie said, patting his chest.

Osman had only a vague idea of these expulsions, but he no longer dismissed them, given that so many people were telling the same general story. "Did they miss Istanbul?"

"Every day of their lives. It killed them early, both of them. My parents were not rich—their parents were—but they were upper middle class at least." Pausing to overtake another driver at speed on Athens's ring road, he continued: "The Turks made life difficult for these Constantinople Greeks by levying taxes, staging boycotts, and using violence with the pogrom of 1955; it reduced their business. Then, in 1964, because my father held Greek nationality, he was deported, and my mom, though a Turkish national, went with him."

"So little of this is talked about in Turkey," Osman muttered loudly enough for the cab driver to hear, but it was as if he were talking to himself.

"Yes, well, living in Greece just about killed them. We had lived in a luxurious apartment in Constantinople and moved into a two-bedroom place in Kallithea, which means 'good view,' but I for one never saw a good view from there."

"I know that from old people in Izmir who used to be, how do you call them, *beys* and *pashas* in Thessaloniki, then they came to Izmir and were poor."

"Yes, exactly, this is what wars and expulsions do: ruin people's lives and teach people that they should not get along. This has been going on forever and probably still will."

Engrossed in the conversation, Osman did not follow the route into Athens. After getting off the ring road, almost Germanic in its efficiency, they entered Kifisias Avenue, and the chaos began. This was clearly one of Athens's main arteries, and it looked like an old, hardened, cholesterol-filled artery: ready to burst, cars everywhere parked illegally. The storefronts were vacant where there were once clearly expensive, high-end boutiques. Racing toward the Hilton, an older Athens of six-to-seven-story apartments appeared, appointed well enough, but also wearing a few years of smog and plenty of fatigue. The US embassy, imposing and well guarded, appeared on the right, and suddenly, the Parthenon and Acropolis came into view.

Osman felt his heart stop, looking at its grandeur. Perched in the center of a sprawling, crawling city, this edifice was easily the most beautiful thing he had ever seen. The cab driver continued his life story and travails, and Osman heard nothing; he just sat and stared at the Parthenon.

Quickly enough, the driver turned to the Athens Hilton, and a liveried and polite doorman opened his door. Osman fumbled for his cash. "Sorry sir, the last part I did not take in; I was looking at the Parthenon. It is amazing."

"Yes, take the walk around the Acropolis. It used to be my father's solace, but it is hardly the walk around Agia Sophia." He sighed, taking Osman's money. "Enjoy your stay, your change is…"

"My change is yours, Sir. I appreciated the drive and the conversation."

His reception, hotel room, and tips were taken care of. And the view of the Acropolis! He sat transfixed for a few more minutes, and then looked at his watch. It was thirty minutes until his meeting. He unpacked and headed for the shower.

Normally showers were a quick affair to conserve hot water, and Osman loved traveling to good hotels where he could linger for a few minutes. For some reason, he always got his best ideas or conclusions in the shower. He had only been in Greece for two hours, and it was hard to draw any first impressions. What surprised him were the constant reminders of Asia Minor and the refugee experience that the Greeks carry.

With this on his mind, he strolled down to the lobby with his briefcase in hand, suited suitably for a business meeting. Arriving two minutes shy of the appointed time, two gentlemen were already waiting at reception. "Mr. Celik? My name is Nondas Kalaitzoglou and this is my colleague Stefanos Karapanos."

Osman could not help but utter a small laugh, which took the Greeks aback. Seeing their reaction, he rushed to explain. "Your surname, with '–oglou,' we have that in Turkish, too. Same with 'Kara–,'" he said with a smile.

"Yes," Nondas replied. "It is common here in Greece, too. The company's founder, my great grandfather, got his start in Smyrna—I mean, Izmir—before he, uh, had to leave for Thessaloniki. That is where the firm got its start, before I moved the offices to Athens about ten years ago, to be, uh, where the action is."

Where is the action, then? thought Osman, but he put on his best game face. "Gentlemen, how about a coffee or tea, or would you prefer lunch? I understand the Byzantine Café here is quite good."

"Sounds good," Nondas replied.

The appetizers were all small talk about families, Izmir, what to see in Athens, and cuisine. The main course was a kleftiko lamb with orzo pasta and a light moschofilero wine and a traditional Greek salad. Because the subject matter and the company were typical of the next nearly two-dozen meetings that Osman would have in the next few days, it makes sense to cover it in detail.

Simonides Enterprises was a company founded in the late 1920s in Thessaloniki, Greece, by a refugee from Smyrna, and was backed by a cousin who had grown wealthy in Argentina. By the 1970s, they had stores in most Greek cities, and a humming factory in the western part of Thessaloniki. With the coming of European integration and generally cheaper imports from elsewhere in Europe, to say nothing of Asia, sales dipped considerably. The 1990s and the opening up of the Balkans offered an opportunity to expand into weak markets with huge pent-up demand. By the year 2000, they had offices in several cities in Serbia, Bulgaria, Albania, Romania, and the Former Yugoslav Republic of Macedonia. Thirteen years later, most of those offices had been closed; the factory moved to Bulgaria, just over the Greek border, and a dozen stores in Greece barely made it through severe discounting. From an eighty-million-euro turnover in 2004, it was down to thirty-three million.

The company was for sale. Of the twenty-three companies he met, eighteen were Greek. Most of the Greek companies had production in Bulgaria or Romania and boasted of their large Balkan network and brand recognition. They all sported executives who were often family members and spoke very good English laced with Britishisms (which Osman despised). The other companies were generally represented by ex-engineers or burly, mafia-looking types whose English was functional, except for one Bulgarian, who was probably fifty years old or so and spoke an English that could easily pass for Midwestern American—"usually a sign of secret police training," he was later told.

Osman's firm was clearly the big fish in the pond, and every other company wanted to do some sort of business with them. This could only serve Osman well, and he reported back to Husayn in detail about his various meetings. Husayn, on the other end of the phone, chuckled ever so slightly.

"Just as I anticipated, they are all takeover targets. Good—we can buy market share, production, and distribution. Meet as many people as you can, and we will invite four or five top candidates to Izmir and Konya for further discussions."

Osman had to hand it to this clever peasant. He had figured out that the opportunities were in acquisition rather than sales. The affable, cosmopolitan Osman was the right guy to start the ball rolling, and Husayn would guide the ball thereafter. Osman realized that Husayn was far from just an opportunist and political crony; he thought many, many moves ahead. And he had an ego as big as Asia Minor, so it made sense to stroke it deftly. "Husayn Bey, I really appreciate your giving me this opportunity. I have learned so much, and I think our company has great long-term opportunities in this region."

"Osman, my boy, you are really catching on to this business. I worried about you in the beginning—too much literature and Western influence—but you are remembering your roots. Your father, a hero of our republic, must be proud of you. In our own way, we are working to reclaim some of the ground and the glory of our empire. You are more than a salesman here: you represent Turkey and Islam."

Thank Allah we are not on Skype, as my eyes are rolling now, though Osman. "Thank you, Husayn Bey."

"Also, do take some time off to explore Greece. Find our past there and make our present. Good evening, my boy!"

"Good evening, Husayn Bey."

It was the third evening of the conference, and Osman was literally shredded with fatigue. He avoided all invitations, called Nilufer,

and turned in early. Nilufer wanted to keep him on the phone forever with questions, but he begged for sleep. He woke up late for the
last day of the conference, showered and shaved, and went to the
lectures. At the first coffee break, while being accosted by a Kosovo
textile wholesaler, he felt a light tap on the shoulder.

"Osman, I am Ebru," she said in English with a busy smile.
Switching to Turkish, she said, "I am here to take you away from
this—at least for a few minutes."

Osman politely but pointedly excused himself, which offended
the Kosovo merchant, but Ebru quickly silenced him in another
language.

Walking away with her, Osman asked, "What did you say, and in
what language?"

"I told him in Serbian that I am your banker and my time is more
valuable than yours," she said with a wicked smile. "That guy looks
more like a drug dealer than a businessman. Steer clear of those
guys." Then turning to him with the full force of her blue eyes, she
asked, "Buy me a coffee?"

"I thought you'd never ask!"

Running into a streetside café, Ebru ordered two coffees in a
Greek that seemed steady, though perhaps not fluent. "Nilufer told
me you are a force of nature! I can see what she meant."

She continued, "Your wife is a gem, Osman: one of those people
who is so much more than she seems. Anyway, my day is booked solid,
so I have two items to cover with you. First, your official business. The
country manager is on standby to meet you for lunch or dinner any
day this week. The second item, which may influence the first, is that
I have arranged a dinner for you tomorrow with some of my friends,
including historians and ethnologists who may be able to assist you
in your quest."

"Do you know about my quest?"

"Yes."

"Nilufer."

Yes."

"It's interesting, she really wants me to find some things out here. It's almost as if she wants to find out some things for herself."

"She does." Her eyes held his.

She broke the gaze, finished her coffee, and got up to leave. "But that's all for now. Say, why don't you let the boss buy you lunch today? The conference is ending early this afternoon, and you can meet me for lunch at, say, 2:00 p.m.? I can have a car sent for you."

"Who can say no to you?"

"Very few people!" she said with a wicked smile. "As for tonight, I will pick you up for aperitifs at 6:00 p.m. Dress smart, but no suit."

The rest of the day passed uneventfully. The conference ended, and everybody made sure to say goodbye to Osman and to drop another card into his hand "in case the previous one had been misplaced."

He had just enough time to drop stuff off in the room before the car would arrive from the bank. When he arrived in the lobby, a man in a black suit introduced himself as the bank chauffeur. They went to a very quiet and lovely restaurant in Kolonaki, a hilltop neighborhood in central Athens with expensive houses and boutiques. The country manager, Mr. Orhan Cetin, was every inch the successful banking bureaucrat.

"Mr. Celik, thank you for taking the time to meet with me," he said, shaking Osman's hand effusively. "I had the pleasure of serving under your father, Colonel Celik, for a time in Diyarbakir. I was just a newly minted lieutenant then."

Ah, ex-military. Well, at least he's not an Erdogan crony, Osman thought. He knew their language because he grew up around it, and he felt more comfortable with them than with "Husayn types."

Cetin suggested they order a white Moschofilero wine, and Osman glady agreed. It was yet another sign they understood each other. The meal was excellent, and Cetin was clearly a good financial partner for any acquisitions that Osman's company might make in Greece. He had also studied in America at American University in Washington, DC, where he got his master's degree in international relations. Cetin had left the army for banking in his midthirties as a major, just as the Turkish economy was reforming in the early nineties. Now in his early fifties, his Greek post was probably a stepping-stone to a preretirement position in Istanbul. He was from Iznik, not far away from Istanbul, and planned to retire on the Sea of Marmara.

Finishing up with a nutty and syrupy dessert, Cetin asked, "What are your plans? Do you return tomorrow to Izmir, or will you stay to see the sights?"

"I will stay in Athens for a few days to see the sights, and then I am actually going south for several days to Monemvasia and Neapolis."

"Interesting choice. I have been to Monemvasia; it has wonderful little hotels. I know you are interested in Ottoman history, but while Monemvasia has some Ottoman ruins, the Mora—the Peloponnesus—has very few Ottoman monuments." Cetin continued authoritatively: "Greece's northern provinces—Macedonia, Thrace, and Epirus—these have the Ottoman monuments, as well as Crete."

"Thanks, I will think about it. I met some Greek tourists in Izmir who insisted that I visit them there."

"I see. Well, then you will probably enjoy yourself. Can I get you back to the hotel?"

"Yes, thank you."

Later that evening, Ebru was seated in a lounge chair, waiting for Osman. She wore a blue blouse and jeans that matched perfectly with her azure eyes. She kissed him on both cheeks and walked out to the doorman, who hailed a taxi. "Osman, the group you will meet is, how can I say, eclectic. Leftists, gays, et cetera. And they are like family to me, so if you have any issue with that, we need to change plans."

Osman was taken aback, both by the comment, but also by the abruptness. "Ebru, why do you tell me this, and like that?"

She stared him straight in the face, to the degree possible in the taxicab. "Experience, Osman. You may be from Izmir, a liberal city, and married to a very intelligent and open-minded woman, but you are still a middle-class Turk and from a military family. Sorry, but that type of man has his hypocrisies, his issues."

"If that is the case, then why am I even here seeking out my long-lost, brother, so to speak?"

"Because Osman," she said, gently and disarmingly, "deep down, you value the truth over your illusions, personal and inherited."

Osman said nothing, just nodded. *Wow, this woman gets it!*

"Speaking of family and hypocrisies, among the people you will meet tonight is my fiancé, a Greek painter from Yannina—that's in northern Greece, near Albania. His family members know of me, but they think that I am a Bosnian Serb from Sarajevo, and therefore Orthodox Christian. His uncle is a bishop of the Greek Church, and the family is very religious and suspicious."

"Who knows the truth?"

"Aside from you and me, the people around the table tonight. That's how it will stay for now."

They ducked into a dive bar in Petralona, an inner Athenian neighborhood with a gritty, working-class environment, including plenty of obvious foreigners: Arabs, Africans, and Pakistanis. At a corner in the bar, five people waited, nursing shots of *ouzo* or beers.

There was Yorgo: a tall, lanky, reddish-haired fellow with a flowing shirt who had studied marketing at George Washington University in Washington, DC, who was as gay as could be. His partner, Stathis, was a historian specializing in Asia Minor Greeks with postgraduate studies in Cambridge and Edinburgh University. Isidoros—a thin, pale fellow with a slight brown beard—got up to kiss Ebru; he was the painter from Yannina. Kosta, a professor from the University of Thrace, was there with his wife, Georgia, who also had a PhD in history, but no job. Unexpectedly, another friend was in the bar: Arben, an Albanian student at the University of Athens, who was working on a dissertation about the Greek War of Independence. It was a real stroke of luck for Osman, though Arben's English was poor.

"So, Osman, how do you like Athens?" Yorgo said after introductions to break the ice on the discussion.

"A pick up line, eh?" said Isidoros, mocking him good-naturedly.

"No doubt it would have worked on your uncle, the bishop, but this fellow is going to take some finessing," Yorgo shot back mercilessly.

Osman had rarely heard such talk in Turkey, at least not in his circles, and he had to say that he enjoyed it. Greeks were more at ease with themselves. Such an exchange in Turkey could easily have gone off the rails.

"Anyway, you are here on business and a personal matter?" Kosta the Thracian professor cut in.

"Yes."

"Is it your first time in Greece?"

"It is, I am sorry to say."

"Well, you have only seen a bit of Athens, so it is hard to make an impression."

"Yes, it seems very familiar, and yet very different. I have lived with stereotypes all of my life. I am from a military family; the histories have been very cut and dry, and, I fear, very one-sided."

"Both sides can be one-sided," Yorgo reminded.

"Yes, I am fortunate that I was a voracious reader of American literature, and I always liked the, how do you say, Anglo-Saxon ability to deconstruct things."

"Well," Kosta reminded him, "the Anglo-Saxons are good at doing that after they screw everything up in the first place. The Americans of Hawthorne or Thoreau's generation wrote of freedom and democracy while they committed wholesale genocide of the native tribes, and now they deconstruct history well after they have reaped the benefits of their ill-gotten gains."

"Point taken, Kosta," Osman said, "but their historiography and literature does deconstruct. Does yours? Our Turkish literature certainly does not. Even our arguably greatest contemporary author, Orhan Pamuk, is constantly in trouble with the State."

Kosta laughed, and so did the others. Sitting back, Kosta admitted, "Well, yes, we do better than you do, but that is hardly a bar to set."

The *tsipouro* arrived with glasses for everyone. Kosta was kind of the don of the group, and poured for everyone. Raising his glass, he said, "A toast for our friend from across the Aegean. No doubt this transparent liquid will assist in greater transparency in our thoughts, which will bring the truth…"

Stathis then interrupted. "…whether the truth shall set us free, is, of course, another matter entirely."

"Truth or Consequences," Yorgo said laughingly. "I remember seeing that name in America; I think it is a town somewhere in Texas or New Mexico. I know that the truth was that I am gay, and the consequences were that my father disowned me."

Stathis put his hand on his partner's shoulder. "Truth has consequences. Once you know, you cannot go back."

"Well," Osman began, "I cannot compare it, but my own father is far from amused about my asking questions about our background. Or about my questioning official Turkish Republic history."

"So," Kosta asked, "Are you really prepared to find things out about your background—things that may change you forever?"

"I am here, aren't I?" Osman said.

"Being 'here' is completely different than being 'ready.' I am not trying to lecture you. I am the grandchild of Pontic refugees on one side, and on the other side, I am a Greek Macedonian with relatives scattered to the four winds of Eastern Europe from the Greek Civil War. I have witnessed things within my father's village, when the truth comes out, that have destroyed lives. Including my father's."

"That is more recent history; I think the history I am looking for is much more distant."

"You may be right, but you never know. Greece and Turkey have been in a deadly embrace for more than one thousand years, and we remain so."

Osman felt a chill up his spine, as if Kosta had sensed something. Ebru broke in, seeking to steer the conversation. "Yorgo, put in a *meze* order. We need to pace the tsipouro with some food."

Stathis took the cue. "Osman, tell us what you know and what you seek."

Osman told his story about meeting Yannis, and his feeling that somehow he had origins in that part of Greece, Monemvasia. He was determined to find out.

Stathis was much more sensitive and indirect than Kosta. "Well, Osman, as you may know, the Muslim population of the Peloponnesus, the Morea or Mora in Turkish, was basically exterminated in the first year or two of the Greek War of Independence. The vast majority of these people were local converts—Greeks or Arvanites—and Albanian speakers. They were often only a few generations converted, and there is evidence that much of the larger-scale conversions occurred after that brief couple of decades of Venetian rule in the Morea from the 1690s to 1715."

"This much I have read from British sources, particularly Sir Steven Runciman, who was rather pro-Greek as sources go."

"Yes. Greek history does acknowledge the extermination of the Morean Muslims. Our national hero, Kolokotronis, said it himself: 'Not a Turk shall remain in the Morea,' and he was as good as his word. In terms of the identity of the times, any Muslim, including a recently converted one, was a Turk. The degree of Turkification, or Islamization, of course, varied greatly, and in remoter areas, a quiet reconversion was possible. There are anecdotes of this occurring, particularly in mountain villages where the population was small and often related across sectarian lines."

"So, it is possible that some Muslims just faded into the population by becoming Christians and Greeks," Ebru said. "That makes sense."

Kosta broke in, "Just as it occurred in the population exchange in the 1920s, particularly in the Pontos on the Turkish Black Sea. Many Greeks simply remained and were shielded by their Muslim neighbors." Looking at Osman directly, he said, "It also occurred in Ionia, in Smyrna, sometimes right under the noses of the Turkish authorities or in collusion with them."

Again, a gentler Stathis broke in, "You know, massacres and expulsions never really succeed. The land never forgets its former occupants, and humanity always registers small triumphs against inhumanity. In the long history of our two peoples, there are both instances of great inhumanity as well as of humanity, and the attempt to separate Greek and Turk into separate, hermetically sealed categories is a foolish endeavor doomed to failure."

Osman asked, "Did any Turks, I mean, local Muslims, escape?"

"Yes, there were Turkish ships that must have broken through the blockade. I have also heard that a group of Morean Muslims who had survived the massacre had settled in coastal Turkey, specifically in Antalya, where they remained a distinct group for a few generations. Lightly Islamicized Greek Cypriots had also been transferred to Antalya after the British took over Cyprus."

Osman nodded furiously. "My father is from Antalya. His father's name was Osman; he named me after his father. And he was named after his grandfather."

"Just like we Greeks do," Kosta said.

"But we Turks do this less often. But my father insisted that I name my first-born son after him. He did not offer any explanation, but just said, 'This is how we do it in the Celik family.'"

Silence.

"Well," said Yorgo, "get that man a beer." Seven beers appeared, but Osman just sat, absorbing.

Ebru sensed Osman's feelings. "Osman, there is no way to know this for sure. It is still conjecture."

"Walk the ground," Stathis said. "Go down to the Morea, to where your 'double' lives, go to his ancestral village, and see what you feel. This is the only way to know."

"Hardly a scientific approach," Kosta said a bit snidely.

"Kosta, this is not a paternity suit!" his wife Georgia broke in. "We are more than just facts and figures; we are feelings. Don't tell me you have never felt connections without or beyond facts."

"OK, I know this," Kosta said. "But he is already predisposed to a theory before he goes there, so his perceptions are clouded by what he has already learned."

"I understand, Kosta," Osman said after he emerged from his almost catatonic state. "But until I met Yannis, my identical twin, I never had any interest in Greece. I considered you the enemy. I feared you as well, as my father does. I am starting to understand why. I feared finding out something, but now I need to understand who I am."

Kosta nodded in agreement, setting down his drink. Looking Osman straight in the eye, he said, "My friend, around this table we are hardly a representative group for Greece." Osman wanted to interrupt, but Kosta held out his hand. "You may find more than you wanted to know, or find that your double, or his family, just don't want to know."

By this time, it was about 11:00 p.m., which was not particularly late for Greece, but Kosta and Georgia were visiting relatives and needed to get back. Yorgo and Stathis also took their leave; they needed to get up for work, but Osman sensed that they could not afford to pay for their share of the inevitable dinner and refused to be invited. Ebru, Osman, and Arben remained. Arben's English was not so good, so he had kept a bit more silent than he might have.

Osman asked both of them to be his guest for dinner, and at a *psistaria* (grill house) on an Athens back street, Ebru asked Arben in Greek his thoughts about the conversation, which his limited English had not allowed him to follow fully. Arben basically validated everything that the others had said. He did offer that there was a fair amount of religious and identity fluidity in those times. Albanian speakers figured prominently on both sides; one battle in the Greek War of Independence was almost exclusively fought between Albanian speakers. "The islands of Hydra and Spetses, where the bulk of the Greek fleet came from, spoke Albanian. Some guerilla leaders would change sides, even midbattle."

"To suggest that there was a highly developed Greek national identity at the time of the War of Independence, either as descendants of ancient Greeks or the Byzantines, is a real stretch of the imagination," Arben said. "Religion served as the primary divider of people in the Ottoman Empire, but even that, particularly in remote areas, was pretty fluid. In outlying areas, aside from the dislocations and disruptions of invasions or plagues, people across religious lines were pretty much all related, and intermarriage, with the female or Christian spouse going Muslim, was not at all uncommon."

"I see," Osman said. "The people at that time: they were probably illiterate, right?

"Of course; probably close to one hundred percent among the women, but at least eighty percent among the men, particularly in the Peloponnesus. This was a remote Ottoman province at the time. The Greeks of the Diaspora in places like Vienna and Odessa; or in Constantinople, Salonika, or Smyrna and certain islands were educated and in contact with the West: these were the ones with the ideas of nationalism, not the local types in the Peloponnesus."

"So, the line between Turk and Greek, or Albanian and Greek, was quite fine?" Osman said.

"They could be from the same human raw material, but religion, education, or experience would ultimately determine what their ethnic identification was."

"And what about some Turks, I mean, local Muslims, escaping by boat? Does that sound plausible?" Osman asked.

"Of course. Why not? You may learn more if you go down to Monemvasia and Neapolis. But be careful. The economy is very bad, and chauvinism is on the rise. This fellow you met: did he seem very... enthusiastic?"

"Well, I have thought about that. I think he is not doing too well financially, and he is, if anything, indifferent. I did not get a great deal of encouragement from him."

"Don't expect too much, Osman. Greeks are a very decent people, but there is a streak of severe xenophobia, and a weirdness vis-à-vis her neighbors. I guess every nation is particularly difficult with their neighbors. I have lived one third of my life in Greece, but I am not particularly welcome here. In Albania I had no religion: my mother was traditionally Orthodox and my father was traditionally Muslim. I was baptized Orthodox here, and that was kind of my 'union card' to acceptance here. Certainly my kids—if I ever get married and have any—will be accepted as Greeks and integrate. But not me, and no matter how hospitable Greeks can be—and often are—there is a line, and as a Turk and a Muslim you fall well on the other side of it."

With that, Arben took his leave. It was just Osman and Ebru now. "How 'bout a nightcap, Osman?"

Settling in to a nearby bar, Osman ordered another beer. "So nice not to wonder who will be counting the number of drinks I have!" He winked.

"Yes, I imagine that in your job particularly, they keep tabs on infidel behavior!" Ebru said, laughing and tossing back her sandy blond curls.

"You seem so comfortable here, in spite of everything Arben and the others said," Osman asked, "How do you do it?"

"Because I am part of here," Ebru said. "When I lived in Sarajevo, it became obvious. I tracked down relatives. My father's parents came from Bosnia, which is why I am fairer than most Turks. The language was spoken in our house along with Turkish, so I had enough to get started there."

"What was Sarajevo like?" Osman asked.

Ebru sighed and pulled on her cigarette. "It was the late 1990s, the war had shredded the town with bombs, bullet holes, poverty. There were real open wounds, both literally and figuratively." Looking at her empty glass, she called the waiter for another round. "I hope you don't mind. I am not a nice Turkish girl. I drink. I smoke. I screw."

"Like I said, Nilufer told me that you are a force of nature," Osman said, just slightly defensively. "So, you were saying about Sarajevo…"

"Yes, I found third cousins there. Many of them had married Serbs or Croats, but some of them fled the country because such 'Yugoslav marriages,' if they survived, suddenly became politically unaccept-able. There were lots of wounded people, physically and spiritually. Lots of brilliant people: scientists, artists, musicians."

She went on. "The city people had all been Yugoslavs for the most part, but the war and its aftermath radicalized a lot of them. Men started wearing long beards; women wore veils. Village people with more radical ideas gained political and economic power and a mafia crony economy emerged, backed by Arab and Turkish money. A local *imam* got me expelled from my job at the Turkish Cultural Center by telling the director that I went around unveiled and out alone with men, including Serbs."

She shook her head, thinking back. "Nothing has been built in Bosnia except mosques and churches: empty, brand-new mosques compete with churches for height, setting, and prestige, and the country sinks ever deeper into poverty and ignorance. Sarajevo had a vibe; I saw it as it breathed its last," she said, pulling heavily on the smoke and inhaling deeply.

"I don't want to live long," Ebru said suddenly. "Nor do I want kids. The human animal does not recognize or respect beauty." Stopping a moment, she said, "Cigarettes, good alcohol, a good lay, staying out all night and working all day is a slow-motion recipe for suicide."

"And now, in Greece?"

"Yes, after Sarajevo the bank gave me an opportunity in Athens. On my first break, I went north to Macedonia province to find my grandmother's birthplace."

"In Greece?"

"Yes, she was a Valaades, a group of ethnic Greek Muslims resid-ing in villages in western Macedonia, particularly around the town of Grevena. Most had converted to Islam in the eighteenth century, but were ethno-linguistically Greek; 'Just an onion skin separates us from the Christians,' went the saying. When the population ex-change came in the 1920s, they were declared Turks because of their religion and had to go. My grandmother and her parents sailed from

Thessaloniki to Izmir. But her older sister was betrothed to a Greek and had converted to Orthodoxy a couple of years before."

"Though other Valades tried to convert at the last minute to avoid expulsion, usually unsuccessfully, those who converted a few years before the exchange were allowed to remain. When I came to my grandmother's village outside Grevena, her daughter (my aunt and my mother's first cousin) welcomed me like her child. I spent three days with her, feeling more at home than I ever did in Izmir or Sarajevo."

"Quite a story," Osman offered.

"A couple of days later, in Grevena, I went shopping with a newfound cousin. We stopped at a café, and sitting next to us was a serious, studious fellow reading in German a book about Viennese painters. It was Isidoros."

"That's how you met him."

"Yes, well we talked all afternoon and evening, and screwed that very night, in his aunt's house there. We got on the bus to Athens the next day, and he has been living with me in my studio ever since."

"And his parents?"

"Well, here is the kicker," she said, tearing up and shaking. "His uncle is a bishop in Yannina, and the family is very religious. So, officially, I am Serbian. This covers the Orthodoxy part. Greeks and Serbs are close, but one of his relatives saw through this when I could not cross myself without making a mistake, so I told them I was raised by strict communists and that I was only now, 'returning to our faith.'" Sighing, she knocked back her drink.

"Another, maestro!" she said, loudly and to the annoyance of the other few patrons.

"But you are engaged; has it been announced?"

"We are engaged, but in this fucking country we can never really make it," she said, now slurring a bit. "The parents had a party for us in Yannina, and of course His Beatitude came."

"What does that mean?"

"The formal address for a high churchman in Orthodoxy. I learned enough to pass muster, and then a neighbor said, 'I have a surprise for you,' and two guys were pushed forward, who greeted me in broken Serbian. They had been with the Greek volunteers serving in the Bosnian Serb forces. One started talking loudly about his exploits against the 'dirty Bosnians' while the other looked away in disgust. I had to sit there and smile through all of this."

"It must have been terrible."

"It was, and I took myself outside, saying I needed air and that the language barrier was hard on me. I felt a hand on my shoulder. It was the other guy who had been in the Bosnian Serb army. 'Your accent,' he said, 'is not native to Bosnia or to Serbia. Where are you from?'"

"I told him the truth. I no longer cared."

"He gently took my hand and said, 'I am sorry you had to hear that. The war was horrible on all sides—what an animal the human is!' It was clear, however, that though Isidoros loved me for who I am, the family would never love me this way, and Greece would never accept me."

"That is kind of what Arben was hinting, isn't it?"

"Look, Osman, you grew up a Turk, an army boy, a class all its own in the modern Turkish Republic," she said in a voice with just a drip of irony. "You are for the first time finding the subtleties in your own background, and it will be jarring."

"Well, I can accept having Greek blood," Osman said, "without an issue."

"I guess you would, after all; you have Nilufer!" she said, with the *veritas* that comes from *in vino*.

"What?"

"What what, Osman?" She looked surprised, "Oh fuck," she said, loudly and luckily in Turkish. "You mean you...don't know?"

"Know what?" Osman demanded, now angry and feeling betrayed.

"Nilufer's mother was Greek, and I don't just mean by blood; she was a...secret Christian."

"Oh my God!" Osman said.

"Yes, quite literally." Ebru said.

Suddenly, dozens of little habits, foibles, and attitudes made sense. Nilufer had always passed as a liberal daughter of the Turkish Republic: secular, modern, and Western, but not too obtrusive and declarative. She was a devoted, playful wife, but at times she insisted on quiet, meditative solitary time, particularly on Sundays. She liked to walk in the old city on Sundays or to visit old family friends that were usually much older and almost reclusive—generally not people Osman had met. Her Sunday walks were legendary, and once her father-in-law, the colonel, said, "Off to Church, are you?" He meant it as a joke, but she burst out crying and refused to talk to the colonel until he apologized, which he did after nagging from Osman. At the time, Osman thought it was the insult that hurt, but it was rather the truth and its being hidden.

"I am so blind," Osman said. "I am a bad, bad husband."

"No you are not; you were not ready to receive it. Stop being tough on yourself."

"But it explains so much, and also why she wanted me to find this out. But how do you know?"

"We are more than just school friends; our families are old friends from the 1920s. When my grandmother's family was expelled from Greece, they occupied a Greek house abandoned by the fleeing Greeks. The neighboring Turkish family had a niece from Ayvalik whose parents, they said, had been killed in the course of the Greek army's retreat from Asia Minor, and they raised the niece as their own. This niece was in fact from Ayvalik, but she was a Greek. Her 'uncle,' our neighbor, had worked for the girl's father and had given his word to protect her—and he did, allowing her to choose her religious affiliation. She was part of a small, tight-knit network of secret Greeks in Izmir, and she found her husband among this same secret community. They were Nilufer's grandparents."

"Orhan and Fatme: I remember seeing their pictures."

"Or Christos and Phaedra, if you call them by their baptismal, Christian names."

"But Baba Faruk, Nilufer's late father: he was a rather devout Turk."

"Yes, Faruk was Muslim and rather observant. His wife, your mother-in-law, was raised with both traditions. But she was Orthodox in her heart." Smiling, Ebru said, "What Greek she learned was from my mother."

"How?"

"Well, remember, my grandmother was from Greek Macedonia, so she passed on some Greek to my mother and me. Further, the Valades family always respected the Virgin Mary, like many Muslims, so we would go to Nilufer's family to pray to her icon. This icon is now in your house!"

"It's complicated," Osman said, thinking about Facebook's relationship status choice.

"It is."

He barely remembered arriving back at the hotel. The next afternoon, still groggy from the food and drink, as well as the overload of information and emotional baggage, Osman woke up late and prepared his checkout from the Hilton. He stopped by the concierge, whom he had spoken to a couple of days before about getting a rental car. The rental agent would arrive in half an hour with the car, the concierge said.

CHAPTER 8

HOMECOMING, AND HOME FRONT

Osman headed north from the Hilton toward the Athens Ring Road. He wanted the simplest route out of town. It was 4:00 p.m., and rush hour was already beginning. Entering the Attiki Odos, Athens's Germanic Ring Road, he pointed the car toward Corinth.

Yannis had been too caught up in personal stuff to pay much attention to Osman's impending arrival. Work was nonexistent, he was quarreling with his ex-wife again, and Sia had been in Athens for well over a couple of weeks to help her sister with the baby, she said, but Yannis wondered whether their relationship had simply run out its energy.

He would not blame her. She was ten years younger than Yannis, with a voracious sexual appetite and too much time on her hands. As a divorced father nearing forty with an irregular income and living in a country in an economic freefall, the last thing he could think seriously about was a relationship. He wondered, out loud, whether Western-style relationships and marriage were going to be another casualty of this economic crisis. At least he could remember some good economic times in his past. What could Sia look forward to?

Looming over everything was the question of Australia: to go or not to go? His uncle had a job waiting for him—a place to stay for free—and no doubt the extremely handy Yannis could earn extra money from odd jobs like painting and construction. He had worked in Australia for a year when he was younger, and he had returned home after his girlfriend (now ex-wife) threatened to dump him. *Great move*, he thought. *By now I would be a citizen, with a house, perhaps a business or a steady job and savings...*

But his angel was his daughter, Maria. She was the only reason he stayed, because the thought of an extended absence from her was more painful than poverty. If he was honest with himself, though, he also did not want to give up on Sia; he missed her more than he chose to admit.

On the other side, there was this rift with Nondas, his cousin and heretofore his closest confidant. The few times that they saw each other after their fight only a cold nod was exchanged, or a word of hello in passing. In a small town such as Neapolis, this was not unnoticed, and a couple of Nondas's friends—heavies who were ex-military and known for fascist sympathies—would have beaten Yannis senseless had Nondas not intervened and said that "if anything happens to my cousin, the same thing will happen to you."

At his mother's small house on the outskirts of town, however, Nondas carefully assembled copies of several black-and-white photos, blurred yet worth a thousand words, to which he added the following:

My Dear Cousin,

I am sorry that I let our very private and very (for me) painful quarrel become public. I assure you that nobody even slightly associated with me will ever come near your door. I remain your cousin and a faithful, loving uncle to Maria. I came into possession of these photos of my father, in bound captivity, before he was murdered by the Turkish invaders of Cyprus. If you see these photos of the uncle you never knew bound like an animal, you will understand why I cannot have a Turk cross my threshold, nor can I ever again cross yours.

With Love,

Nondas

This came a day before Osman was due to arrive, and in his haste between Daddy duties and odd jobs, he did not have time to open the pictures, and frankly, he did not want to see them. A few hours after the parcel arrived, Osman phoned to tell him when he was arriving. Yannis booked him a room in the one hotel still open in the off-season and got back to work, trying to get as much done as possible before the enigmatic visitor arrived.

Somewhere near the Megara turnoff on the way south, a small, older-model Volkswagen Polo passed Osman's rented Golf at full speed; all Osman saw was a feminine flash of bushy black hair and a cigarette in a pair of full lips. His heart raced for a moment—one of those busy moments of attraction that subsides just as quickly. I guess I miss Nilufer, he thought, and he wished she could be here with him, for she was sagacious.

It was late afternoon by the time Osman had crossed the Corinth Canal, and the motorway to Tripoli would take another hour. He thought to stop in Nauplion, which some tourist guides dubbed the prettiest city in Greece, with lots of architecture from late-Ottoman Greece and the Revolutionary period. Maybe it would be good to take some photos for his cover story to Husayn: searching for the Ottoman heritage of the Peloponnesus!

Not now, he thought, *I need to get to Tripolis, make it an early night, and then set out for Neapolis.* The motorway, dubbed Chicago Avenue by some due to the number of Chicago Greeks who hailed from the area, cut through mountains with a series of tunnels, a clear material legacy of the European Union structural funds. Tripoli he also had to see, for it was the scene of the Greek revolutionaries' greatest massacre of the Muslim Peloponnesian population, including, he was certain, some of his forebears.

The same night Osman spent out with Ebru's friends, Nilufer spent talking to her father-in-law. She put the kids to bed early and began to watch one of the latest, greatest Turkish soap operas in the ex-Ottoman space, from Basra to Bosnia, when the colonel appeared. Damn Turkish parents—they never announce or ask if you want company!

"Welcome, Baba," Nilufer said dutifully.

"Thank you, daughter. Good evening to you. Are my dear grandchildren sleeping?"

"They are, Baba. May I offer you something to drink?"

"May I have some of Osman's secret raki? He never offers me any."

"Oh come now, Baba, you know you are always welcome to it. Would you like a loukoum or water with it?"

"Please, Nilufer."

She set a placemat with plates of loukoum and meze, and sat down across from him.

"And, daughter, please bring in the glass of wine you were drinking. This is your home, and you are the commanding officer here! Your health and that of my grandchildren," he said before downing a shot. "Osman, he is still in Greece?"

"Yes, the conference went well. Our products are in demand, and it will assist his position in the firm."

"Excellent. If the conference ended, why has he not returned?" the colonel asked with narrowed eyes.

"He is traveling around Greece a bit to get to know the market," Nilufer said weakly and defensively.

The colonel shook his head. "You know, daughter, I just don't get my son and his foreign obsessions. First, it was America. OK, I get that: a superpower rich and full of freedom and whatever. OK. And let's face it, America has been a very useful ally." Nilufer did not like the way that he said *useful*. "But by the Prophet, what is this new obsession with Greece? A useless country: always in debt, weak, but strong, and sneaky enough to stir the pot. They ruined the Ottoman Empire and stirred up the others as well. They might have ruled, right here, had Atatürk not thrown them all into the Aegean."

Nilufer shuddered here, and the colonel softened a bit. "I know it sounds barbaric to you: a nice middle-class Turkish girl born in the

1970s, but our republic has had a rough life, with enemies all around and within."

She sat, stonefaced, and the colonel poured himself another. Nilufer just stared at him. A minute passed, then another. "Daughter, do you want to say something? Because you look like you do!"

"Baba, do you?"

"What do you mean?"

The colonel downed the shot, slowly getting up. "Daughter, I have tired you. Women bore easily with talk of history."

He went to the door, not waiting for Nilufer's muffled wishes for a good evening.

CHAPTER 9

"YOU MUST LEAVE HER, CHRISTOS!"

SMYRNA, LATE SEPTEMBER, 1922

Phaedra's fever had not subsided. The heavy French thermometer read nearly forty degrees Centigrade. Outside, Smyrna was in chaos, the Greek army having upped anchor and left in haste after the crushing defeat dealt to it by Kemal Atatürk's ragged but deadly Turkish nationalist army. The Smyrna quay was a sea of dying humanity as people burned by the fire sought solace by drowning; pregnant women were dying in childbirth while their children lived but minutes, and all this happened in sight of the warships of several European powers and the United States! Greece's World War I allies watched in close proximity as fire and sword worked genocide on Smyrna's Greeks and Armenians.

Those who chose to hide in Smyrna, whether in their homes or with others, were rooted out by marauding Turks who were either soldiers or locals eager for revenge.

Christos Liparidis was the head of one such family of huddling refugees. A moderately prosperous fruit merchant from Aivalik, he had traveled south to Smyrna with his family just before the Greek administration collapsed to collect debts and to arrange for transport to mainland Greece. Christos was a good businessman, but he had a lousy nose for politics and the way the wind was blowing. That he had debts to collect in Smyrna was one thing, but how could he have brought his family into the eye of the storm, when a quick caïque trip could have brought the whole brood to the nearby Greek island of Lesbos? The Turkish army might be unstoppable, but they could not compete with the Greek navy; the islands would not fall to the Turks, but by the summer of 1922, notwithstanding idiotic assurances by the Greek occupation authorities in Smyrna, Aivalik and elsewhere, it was clear that the Greek occupation enterprise on the Asia Minor mainland was doomed.

Now, in Mehmet's cellar, he could only bang his head against the wall. *How could I have been so stupid? We are simply waiting to be caught and killed, and there is no aid in sight. Even if we get to the quay, there are no ships, and we will wait to die of hunger and thirst while our women and children are violated...*

And speaking of children, there was his youngest, Phaedra, felled by a fever in the crowded city and convulsing. Medicines had disappeared from the shelves, and Mehmet's wife Pinar had used up all of their vinegar with various remedies.

But this situation could not go on. Any minute, the Turks could arrive at Mehmet's door, thus far inviolable because he was Turkish and known to support the Turkish nationalist cause. His eldest two boys, seventeen-year-old Mustafa and nineteen-year-old Ibrahim, had fled east to join the Turkish nationalist forces. His daughters by Pinar were younger—eight and six. His first wife died birthing Mustafa. Ibrahim was killed in the Battle of Afyonkarahisar leading a charge against the Greek lines.

Mehmet came down to the cellar again.

"Christos, if I could do it any differently, I would, but you must leave. Freighters are coming to the port now to ferry off refugees. To stay here will mean death for you and me, and poverty and disgrace for my family." This was not a debate; it was a demand.

"But Phaedra cannot travel; she must remain." When Christos moved to protest, he held up his hand. "I swear by Allah no harm will come to her. I will protect her with my life and trade it if need be; come what may."

"How can you ask me to leave my daughter behind?"

"Because I want her to live, and I want you to live." Sighing heavily, he said, "Anadolu has no place left for Greeks now. We are in a war of extermination. Your army lost, and now the Rums will be eliminated, just as Muslims will be expelled from Greece. This is bad because so many of us lived together under the Sultan's peace. His rule is no more; the empire is no more. You made Greece; we will make Turkey. You must go."

Christos's lips trembled, whether in rage or terror Mehmet did not know. Mehmet softened a bit. "We did business for years; I know that I owe you money and that you came to town to collect. You are a fair man, always extending me credit and never showing any animosity against me because I am Turkish."

Christos nodded, as if to say, "And now what?"

"I will try to get you down to the quay. I am a known nationalist with a son who is a martyred hero of the new republic." He paused, misty remembering his lost son. "Beyond there you are on your own, but your daughter will be my responsibility. If you get out, you will eventually send me greetings through mutual contacts. Should I receive these, I will find a way to get Phaedra to you."

Christos, feeling the Fates closing in on him, asked the obvious question: "And if not?"

"I have connections; I will forge an identity for her as an orphaned Turkish girl. Allah only knows how many orphans this war has made. It is hardly an implausible story."

Sensing also Christos's final objection, he rested a hand on the poor man's shoulder. "She will remain Christian. I will not interfere with her relationship with Allah. And as for the sums I owe you, they will be hers."

Christos nodded. "We will leave at dusk."

Mehmet lead Christos and his family down to the quay, but the law of the jungle reigned there. Turkish bayonets kept him at bay. He saw the family disappear in the crowd, but did not see the Turks who pocketed the gold sovereign he used to buy them in and then chased after the well-dressed Christos, thinking that the man might also have some sovereigns on him.

He did not see them chase Christos, bayonet him, and then drag his wife and daughter aside. He did not know that Christos's son, distraught at the loss of his mother, father, and sisters, and delirious with hunger, wandered aimlessly and was crushed by the horde of refugees rushing onto the freighter.

Mehmet only knew that, after several years, he had no word from Christos or anyone from his family. Meantime, Phaedra had grown attached to Mehmet and Pinar, and her younger sisters looked up to her with deep sisterly love. She of course knew she was Greek and Christian, but she had the sense to keep her private identity that way, and Mehmet honored his word to Christos to the letter.

Phaedra, now known as Fatme, had her own room in Mehmet's large home, where she kept a chest containing some of the mementos of her past. Her two younger sisters were not allowed to open the closet where she kept the chest, which contained a beautiful icon of the Virgin Mary, given to her by her godfather on her Name Day when she was five years old, together with a photograph of her parents and several other heirlooms.

There was not much to keep. The Turks had looted her ancestral home in Aivalik, and most likely, it was taken over by Cretan or Lesbos Muslims expelled by the Greeks into Turkey. Fatme was recast as a young Turkish girl orphaned by the war—one of so many at the time. Many families took orphans in as domestic help and often adopted or saw to their futures. It merited little attention, and nothing in particular set Fatme off from any other girl in Izmir. She got a very basic education: enough to read and do figures. Notwithstanding Kemal Atatürk's emancipation of women, they were still to be seen and not heard, and this silence served its purpose.

For many years until her late teens, her Christian identity was essentially was a solo experience. The icon, a few prayers, maybe remembering her parents', and her own, Saint's Day. Not being from Izmir, she did not know where the former churches were, and of course the

Greek Quarter had been put to fire and sword, and most of its buildings were destroyed. Though she did not use Greek regularly, she did not forget the language, because many Cretan and Macedonian Muslim deportees from Greece arrived in Izmir and the surrounding villages, and Cretans especially kept their language. Though she found the Cretan dialect difficult to understand, she would often linger when she heard it on the street.

One day, in 1928, she happened to be near the old Greek Quarter when she saw a distinguished-looking, well-dressed, unveiled woman walking alone along the ruins of the area. Fatme followed, though from a distance.

Stopping in front of a courtyard now covered in soot from the fire and collapsing on itself, the woman quickly crossed herself—and suddenly turned to find Fatme not ten feet from her. Startled, she immediately regained her composure, reminding herself of who she was. "What do you want, you little bitch? Following me around?"

Fatme was scared; this woman was at least ten years older than her and very sure of herself. By her clothes and manners, you could tell she was from a rich and important family: not a local Smyrna-merchant type, but rather a member of the Turkish Republic's new class. Tears started to flow. "I am sorry! I saw something I should not! Please let me run away; I'll never tell!"

Suddenly a look of understanding and mild alarm passed over the older woman's face. "I see; we cannot talk here. Follow me." Switching to Greek, a local dialect more like her native one, she firmly but softly repeated, "Follow me, and don't pretend you don't understand!"

Fatme was found out; they got onto a larger street, in a park just off a busy street, where traffic and running kids would drown out their conversation. They spoke to each other in Greek.

"You know the sign of the cross?"

"Yes. *Efendim.*"

"You don't have a Cretan or a Macedonian accent. You are from Ionia. You got left behind?"

"Yes. I was too sick to travel." Fatme was terrified; she was handing her life to this unknown but obviously powerful woman.

"You and I are now sisters, bound by a secret," the older lady said. "I am the wife of a Turkish colonel. He saved my life. I became his wife, but I remain Christian in my private life."

Fatme nodded. "My father—my adopted father—allows me the same thing. I pray to Panagia and he respects this."

"He is a good man, obviously. In the past, this was not unusual. Many Muslims had Christian wives who would remain Christians—even Sultans." She shot Fatme a look. "Many of us are left behind."

Fatme nodded. "I just knew it! You would hear it in people's voices—expressions!" She thought of all the furtive glances, conversations started and then stopped, and it became clear.

The older woman put a hand to Fatme's cheek. "The land never forgets its people. Ionia is our land. There are many of us secret Christians. Some of our people also switched to the Frankish[20] faiths." The older woman stood up and straightened her well-tailored, modern dress. "Today is Sunday; at this time in the early morning you will often find me here. We can go for walks together. I walk around the ruins of the churches. Sometimes I see others: usually women who are often the wives of well-known Izmiris, and only a few men. And of course, the men don't talk to us; it is not done." She thought for a moment. "Do you speak French? I will teach you French on our walks; that will be our excuse."

From then on, when she wasn't with her foster family, she spent every possible hour with the older woman, Muge (Maria). The ruse of French lessons was a convenience, but Mehmet saw through it, saying, "Daughter Fatme, I love you. Allah is one: find Him based on your tradition."

Meantime, through Muge, she also became friends with a refugee family from Greek Macedonia: Valaades Muslims who prayed to the Virgin Mary in spite of their titular Islamic faith. It allowed

---

20 Frankish or Frank refers to the Western European civilization or culture. Turks, Greeks, and occasionally other Balkan peoples use the term to refer to Western (Catholic or Protestant) Europeans. It is rarely used any longer.

Fatme further chances to practice her Greek, and given their devotion to the Virgin, she often lent them her icon—after a decent interval of friendship—and this began a tight bond that would last three generations.

Women marry young in Turkey, and Fatme was nearly twenty. Suitors approached Mehmet and Pinar, but the couple politely turned away most of them, leading some to believe that they were impossible snobs or that Fatme may have had some hidden ailment.

Eventually Muge intervened. A young man—also an orphan—had supported himself in Izmir for years after his parents had been killed in Aydin. His name was Faruk Ozturk. He worked as a longshoreman in Izmir port: a job that, given the reduced commerce of the port, was hardly remunerative. Faruk happened to be Muge's third cousin. His real name was Christos, and his family members in Aydin were killed in their homes and never made it to Izmir. Christos/Faruk had always like to play hide and seek; he was famous in the town for making his parents crazy searching for him. This talent saved his life, and he lived in hiding for the two months of August and September 1922 until the massacres subsided.

He made his way to Izmir, knowing that he stood a better chance of survival in the big city than in Aydin. He lived on scraps, wits, and occasional charity. He was physically strong and tough, and the destroyed city had need of a strong back—this was enough to get him a meal and a place to sleep. He was twenty in 1928—close to induction age for the army—when fate intervened. He saw Maria, his older cousin, walking the Izmir seafront with her Turkish officer husband.

He shadowed Maria for days before finally approaching her in a crowded bazaar, head down, and handing her a written message in Greek: "It is me, Christos." He waited at the end of the bazaar, and then walked slowly as Muge/Maria followed. In a wooded area, having made sure that nobody was around them, he approached her without embracing her, knowing that eyes might still be following the well-dressed wife of a republican officer.

She stood, motionless, staring at this wiry, muscled man in ragged clothes who was the only link to her past and lineage. Tears flowing, she embraced him without care of prying eyes or convention, sobbing so loudly that anyone within earshot would have turned their heads. After a few minutes, which shed years of tension and pain, she suddenly regained her senses, especially her sense of smell, as the stench of Christos's ragged clothes reached her tear-covered nostrils.

She pulled away, straightened her tailored Western suit and skirt, and tried to regain her composure. "How did you survive?"

"I hid in the mountains north of town and made my way to Smyrna on back roads months after the massacre," he said flatly. "Once the smoke and the smell of burning flesh stopped, I went into town."

What could she do for him? He was a mess: ragged and wild, both from several years of living basically homeless, but also, she remembered, from before. His family was very poor and rough; his father, her mother's cousin, was a barely solvent farmer who spent most of his time hunting to supplement his tiny plot. For him, Greek rule in Aydin was a chance to settle economic as well as political scores. He fought against the Turks, and his role earmarked him for death when the Turkish regulars, and local guerillas, took the city from the Greeks. The guerillas killed the whole family: Christos's and hers. Of seventy family members, nearly all of them were killed except her—and now him—aside from the many who may have escaped to Greece.

But what could she do now?

Very little. She could hardly welcome a strange young man into the house. Her husband had covered her origins, but he would have trouble explaining a second lost relative, and hosting a man of Christos's youth and physique in the house as a nonrelative was simply not done. There was not an easy solution. She surreptitiously passed him some liras and agreed to meet him again in the same place, on certain days, when and if eyes were not around.

A couple of months later, she jumped upright from a sound sleep. "Of Course! Phaedra!" She needed a husband, and Christos needed a wife. Both wanted to remain Christian, at least in their home life.

Muge/Maria approached Phaedra/Fatme with the idea. Phaedra agreed in principle: she knew she had to get married, and she realized that there were few chances to marry a secret Christian. Muge took Fatme on a walk down by the old Greek Quarter, silently pointing to the potential spouse. Muge had passed some money to Christos/ Faruk to buy a suit and to get cleaned up, and with his new scratchy wool suit and a clean shave from an expert Izmiri barber, he cleaned up well enough. Both signaled their interest in pursuing the matter.

How to approach Fatme's parents was not so simple. They were a comfortable middle-class merchant family with a martyred officer son and another son who was a War of Independence veteran and an official in Ankara. Faruk was clearly of a lower socioeconomic class. People would talk.

Muge here came to the rescue by finding Faruk a job at the port through her husband's connections, and Faruk's merchant father-in-law also helped in getting Faruk established as a proper husband for his foster daughter. Some tongues clicked that maybe the quick and quiet marriage ceremony was the result of some "dishonor" that the unveiled, liberal Fatme had brought on the family, but after some time and Faruk's diligence in his work, any thoughts of this faded.

Faruk and Fatme raised three children, one of whom—a green-eyed girl named Ayse—married a quiet Turkish Muslim accountant, named Faruk. One of their children was a lively girl named Nilufer, who was born in 1975.

CHAPTER 10

HOMELAND

He arrived in the late afternoon when the sun had fallen behind the craggy mountains of the Mani: the middle finger of the southern Peloponnesian Peninsula that was the domain of guerillas for more than a thousand years. This rough, rocky peninsula was never really conquered by the Turks, and at times it acted as an independent, clan-based chiefdom that was dependent on piracy and brigandage. The Maniot warriors, in fact, were the first group to raise the standard of rebellion against the Turks, and in turn committed some of the worst excesses against their Muslim neighbors.

Neapolis was a coastal town with ten thousand inhabitants at the most. It was basically one coastal road with a few taverns, shops, cafés, schools, and municipal offices. There was a small pier that was mostly for transit to nearby Elafonissos and the more distant, larger island of Kythera. It was the kind of place, as they say, "Where you could not get to third gear in on your car from one end to the other." Yannis was waiting at a waterfront tavern as promised. Osman pulled up and parked nearby, walking in to greet Yannis.

"Welcome Kardesh Osman!" Yannis said, using the Turkish word for brother.

"*Adelfe*[21] Yannis, thank you." They embraced heartily.

---

21 *Kardesh* is brother in Turkish, and *Adelfos* is brother in Greek.

"I had to be here to greet you, but I must go quickly to drive some firewood to a nearby village; it's part of my job. I will be back soon. Are you hungry? If so, Georgios here will feed you; if not, we can go to Billinis's Café, and you can have a coffee, maybe a shot of raki, and a sweet."

"OK, can I drop off my stuff at the hotel?"

"Your room is not prepared yet. I told them that I want a suite for you; they need to prepare it. It will be another hour or two." He looked at his watch. "Let's walk your luggage over there, and you can hang out for a drink at Billinis's Café; it is the local hangout. I should be back in a couple of hours."

The proprietor of Billinis's Café welcomed the "other Yannis," and set him down at a table for coffee, a shot of tsipouro, and delicious syrupy cakes. There was no question of paying, and to kill time, he read messages on his Blackberry. Two hours just passed…

He felt a presence rushing toward him, and before he could turn around he was caught in a lustful embrace; lips smacked against his. Deftly, the woman shifted the chair and jumped on his lap, pushing against him and murmuring words in Greek with her hot breath between kisses.

"No, wait, I'm not…" he struggled in English.

In Greek, Sia said, "What up, you drunk?" Billinis, seeing the situation, started toward them to explain. At the same moment, Yannis strode in.

Again, red with embarrassment and perhaps, arousal, Osman said again, "I'm sorry, I am not Yannis; I am his friend, Osman, from Turkey."

"What the fuck are you talking about?" she said in good English. "Yanni, are you fucking with me? If you want me to leave, just say so, you stupid old fuck!" Tears welled up in her eyes.

Yannis ran over to Sia to take her in her arms. She screamed when she saw him: the exact mirror image of Osman. Yannis reached out to embrace her, and she pushed his hands away. "What is this, you have a twin? You didn't tell me about this, what?" Then she stopped and thought for a moment. "Were you sickos double-teaming me? You sick bastards, I'm out of here!" she said, slapping him fast across the face.

"Sia, he is not my brother; he is from Turkey." He grabbed her to keep her from going. He pleaded with Osman, "Osman, do you have identification—a passport?"

Fumbling as quickly as possible, he pulled out his passport and showed the picture page to the now-restrained Sia. "Look, Miss, here I am; I don't speak Greek."

She grabbed the Turkish passport with identification in Turkish and English and slowly set it down on the table. "OK," she said, fumbling for words. "I am sorry, Mr. Osman. What could I have thought?" Then, turning to Yannis, she said, "For God's sake, Yanni, why didn't you mention this?"

"I told you about it briefly: that when I was in Turkey, I met someone who looked exactly like me."

She nodded. "Yeah, I remember it vaguely."

"Look, too much was going on: your sister needed you in Athens, there was the whole question about whether to go to Australia, everything. This was forgotten." Then, turning to Osman, he said, "Good thing she didn't find you in my house; you would have had some explaining to do with your wife."

Sia laughed, embracing Yannis. "Well, Osman, nice to meet you!" She laughed. "I would shake hands, but seeing as we have already kissed, it would be a bit of a let-down!"

Osman turned red with embarrassment, but he said, "It is nice to formally meet you."

There was a quick beep on Yannis's cell phone. "Your room is ready, Osman. We will have dinner at my aunt's house; she wants to meet you and she is the family, how do you say, encyclopedia."

Looking over at Sia, he said, "I am so happy you came back, my love!" He kissed her gently, but deeply.

Sia smiled and gently pulled away. "I have my stuff in my car. Can I move back in?"

"Your home is our home, Sia. I have missed you terribly."

"Do you need a hand?"

"No. It is two suitcases and my laptop. Take care of Osman," she said with a smile that glowed with love.

Osman and Yannis walked to the hotel. "Listen Yannis, if I am intruding on your reunion with Sia, I…"

"Don't think about it. She came back, and that is what counts. Besides, she will probably find your story interesting."

After walking two blocks, they arrived at the hotel: one like so many in Greece, particularly the coastal areas, built like an Athenian apartment block with large balconies and chipping concrete. The hotel was built in the 1970s, when much of Greece was a large construction area, and there was direct hydrofoil service from Athens to Neapolis. That ended in the late 1990s, and since then, aside from some regulars from Northern Europe and more intrepid types, as well as Greeks from the Diaspora, the hotel lacked clientele and investments in upkeep were minimal.

Osman had seen similar hotels in Turkey: concrete structures that were functional, but with cut corners and broken fixtures. He thought to take a shower. Bad idea: the water was cold and just got colder as time went on, despite the handle being all the way on red. He held his breath, soaped himself down, and immediately rinsed off. *Just like Turkish hotels, for the most part*, he thought, shivering.

He quickly went down to what passed for a lobby, where Yannis waited in a fresh white shirt, jacket, and jeans. Osman studied the difference. Yannis was him, but earthier, leaner, tougher. Sia was in the car with a wide smile that Osman remembered from the old days, when love was fresh and unfettered.

Yannis had a Jeep Cherokee: an American model he bought off a repatriated Greek American. "You can tell because the speedometer is in miles rather than kilometers. A Greek American from my village brought it here under a tax-free loophole for the Diaspora, and then sold it to me after a few years. It drinks petrol like a drunk, but when weather hits up in the mountains, it is a lifesaver. It also tows more than European trucks."

Yannis's aunt Matina lived in a house just outside the town in a fertile field on the road toward Falakro, a hilltop village sparkling in the dark distance. Aunt Matina was the town's history teacher, a graduate of the University of Patras, and an authority on the region's history. She and her pensioner husband were big readers and collectors of antiquities, which were displayed lovingly throughout the house.

Matina and Yorgos, her husband, welcomed Osman as family. "My God, he has our look; his face is so much our type! It is uncanny, and something tells me it is not coincidental." As they plowed through an ouzo with seafood meze, a Greek salad, and grilled lamb chops with potatoes—Matina made sure not to use pork—she went over highlights of the region's history.

"As you probably know, Osman, the Morea—the Peloponnesus—has a very, very long history. Five thousand years. Right off the southern cape of the Vatika Peninsula, they have discovered an ancient city just off the coast, though fishermen have known of it for centuries." Osman nodded as Yannis and Sia, but primarily Sia, translated Matina's monologue.

"Now, I know you are interested in the post-Byzantine era, more specifically, the time around the Greek War of Independence in the 1820s. The Turks conquered this part of the Peloponnesus after the Fall of Constantinople in 1453. To be specific, it was in 1460 that Mystra was surrendered to Mehmet the Conqueror, though Monemvasia held out a bit longer. No matter." She then pulled deeply on her cigarette. "The area, however, had changed hands a fair amount even before then. The Slavs invaded the Byzantine Empire, and pockets of Slav speakers remained unabsorbed even up to the Turkish era, though they were Orthodox and Byzantine in identity. The Crusaders had conquered much of the area, along with the Venetians, from 1200 to 1300, and left their own architectural and genetic imprint, particularly the Venetians." Pausing to draw on her shot of ouzo and stub out her cigarette, she said, "You will see many clearly Italian origin names here."

"Anyway, the Venetians also held the area for a few years later on, once again, from 1699 to 1715 officially. Their administrative capital was Nauplion, which was also the first capital of independent Greece."

"I wanted to go there," Osman added. "I am told it is a very pleasant town, and it remained in the style of the 1830s; there is even a mosque there still."

"Yes," Matina said. "It's probably the only Ottoman religious or cultural monument that survives in the whole Peloponnesus. It wasn't just the Turks that were eliminated, but their monuments, too." She paused, thinking for a moment, "like the Taliban who blew up the Bamiyan Buddhas, or those people in Iraq, blowing things up."

There was a bit of silence in the room before Osman broached the subject. "Actually, that kind of leads us to the subject at hand. Is it possible that my people were descendants of refugees from the, um, massacre of the Muslims?"

Matina sighed a little, gestured to Yannis to pour her a drink, removed yet another cigarette from her silver-engraved *tabakera*, and gently tapped the cigarette butt against the table. "A nasty business—not the first or last massacre, but certainly an ugly one."

Sia translated this, a bit confused, and added: "I didn't learn this in my history classes."

Yannis added here: "Until I watched the television documentary *1821* I did not know, either. The history of our revolution is full of glory." Shrugging his shoulders, he said, "I was never that much of a reader, and most of our books—at least the stuff we were supposed to read for school—didn't talk about that."

Osman added, "Well our history was full of your massacres, but a bit scarce on ours. In Turkey, focusing on our own atrocities is, well, hazardous to your health…"

Matina's English was not good, but she understood Osman's last piece, and said in Greek, "Official history anywhere is usually *bullshit*," with the last word in English.

"OK," Matina said, "Let's get back to your question." Drawing on the cig, she began: "The local Turks in the southern Peloponnesus were generally just that—locals who converted to Islam. In other words, Greeks, or Arvanites, who are essentially Greek. The biggest wave of conversions occurred late, actually, after the Turks reconquered the area from the Venetians. Usually they were the wealthier classes who were anxious to preserve privileges in an increasingly corrupt and dangerous Ottoman Empire. They were never more than ten percent of the population here, so there were about fifty thousand at the beginning of the revolution. They usually lived in the cities: places like Mistra, Nauplion, Tripoli, Patras, or Monemvasia, and places with good defenses and communications."

"How about in our village, *Thia* Matina?" Yannis asked, sensing this was Osman's question.

"Well, remember, our village now is almost deserted, with maybe ten permanent residents: old people and people like you, who tend an ancestral house, maybe some fruit trees, et cetera. But it used to be much larger—maybe one hundred families at that time."

"At the time of the revolution?" Osman asked.

"Yes, around that time, and even after. It was high enough in the mountains to dissuade authorities or pirates from attacking. A town of this size may have had a Muslim component, and every source I have, mostly from oral histories, says this."

"So, no real documents?"

"Not really—not until after the revolution. Remember, at the time of the revolution, literacy, particularly outside of the cities, was practically nonexistent, aside from priests or imams or Turkish bureaucrats. In a high mountain village, it is unlikely there were any officials, and even questionable if there were religious figures."

"So it is all, how can we say, speculation?" Osman asked, anxiously.

"Not at all!" Matina insisted. "In fact, oral histories may be more accurate, though more dramatic, than official histories."

Yannis broke in here. "I am taking you up there tomorrow, to the Upper Village, weather permitting; it is getting a bit irregular."

"Right," Matina broke in. "There is nothing like walking the ground, feeling what you feel there. If you go there, you will know."

She got up from the table, went over to a credenza, and pulled out a loose-leaf file folder with a photocopy inside. "If you are from this family, then these individuals are your great-great-great-great-uncles, and our direct ancestors."

Osman and Yannis looked at the copy of the document, holding it up to the light. It was handwritten; even Yannis could barely make it out. "OK, what does it say?"

"It is a church document dated 1836. Our direct ancestor was the son of a Muslim father and a clearly Christian mother, judging by her name." Looking at Osman, Matina said, "There is little likelihood that you are a direct lineal descendant." After her words were translated, she saw his brow furrow slightly. "But—and this is critical—he could have had a brother who escaped before the massacre."

"By ship?"

"Yes, over land is unlikely. A young person would have a hard time walking through all of Greece to Turkey. A Turkish ship could do it in a couple of days, and there is evidence that some Turks, I mean, local Muslims, did escape by ship—particularly before Hydra and Spetses, the two Greek naval islands, joined the revolution. There was a small window of time."

Pulling on the last of her cigarette, Aunt Matina reminded: "As I said earlier, to call these people Turks is to use the terminology of the Ottoman Empire. They were, for the most part, lightly converted Greeks." She stubbed out yet another cigarette and fumbled for the cigarette case. "After the brief period of Venetian rule from the 1690s to 1715, many Greeks converted to Islam. This would mean that our ancestor's family—and possibly yours—had been Muslim for less than one hundred years."

Osman thought for a moment, "Wasn't there a...you know, a stigma attached to leaving Orthodoxy?"

"A loaded question, and one that we, from the distance of nearly two hundred years, do not have the right to decide." Thinking during a puff, she said, "There was likely an economic or political benefit to conversion. In any era, it's about the cash and the perks. It is possible that our ancestor was one of the wealthier people in the area; perhaps his family had made money under the Venetians and conversion would have allowed them to keep their properties."

"So, in other words, Aunt Matina, the revolution was…economic?" Yannis said, clearly crestfallen.

"You are getting ahead of me, Yanni, but, well, sort of," Matina said. "But let me finish first, son. The revolution breaks out in Kalamata and the Mani, just to the west of here. Muslims are being put to the knife, our ancestor probably was not going to wait to be killed, and took off with his children—at least two of them—to Monemvasia. The fortress was impregnable, particularly because the Greek revolutionaries lacked artillery and, until Hydra and Spetses joined the fray, a strong navy."

"Turkish ships may have supplied the fortress and harbored refugees," Osman offered.

"I believe so, Osman, my boy, but you would be able to find that out in your own country better than us." Matina said. "Where in Turkey was your father from?"

"He was from Antalya, a bit east of Rhodes, on the coast."

"Many generations?"

"Back at least one hundred fifty years or so. My father was certain, but he did not elaborate. In fact, he never talked much about his family history, saying simply, 'I am a Turk and proud of it.'"

"Did you think he was evasive?" Matina asked, sensing the answer.

"Defensive and…yes, defensive and evasive," Osman said, with a definitiveness in his voice. "In fact, I would say angry, too, if I ever speculated on our origins." Looking at Yannis, he said, "He was particularly dismissive and upset when I mentioned meeting Yannis, who resembled me so."

"I think he must have known something."

"He should have known; he had a massive library of Turkish history books—all in Turkish. Most of the stuff is very official stuff, usually from the military archives. He is a retired colonel. He may have been deep in denial, but he is not stupid. It had to have crossed his mind."

Matina nodded knowingly, "I see, my son."

"I had heard from independent Turkish historical sources and from historical experts in Athens that there had been a small group of Greek Muslims settled in Antalya. My father would have known this, but I only found out about it in the course of preparing for my trip. We had a fight about my trip to Greece and my questions about my background." He stopped for a minute, and then chuckled. "By the way, my wife: she is part Greek, and she grew up surrounded by Crypto-Christians."

Yannis stopped before translating. "Are you serious? Did you know?"

"Well, Yannis, you know, it is easy after the fact to put the clues together, but no, I did not know." He added, "Look, she was very liberal, but that is typical of Izmir girls, and she has roots in the area for so many generations. She did not like nationalism, and she generally winced at my father's tirades against Greece or his war experience in Cyprus. But she did not like his rants against Kurds, Arabs, or Bulgarians, either, or for that matter, my deep interest in American literature or culture."

Yannis asked, "But why did she never tell you?"

Osman sighed. "It bothered me when I first heard it—less than a week ago, in fact—from her childhood friend." He thought for a moment. "I felt betrayed, but I thought of her patient wisdom combined with a fair sense of irony, and I think she just figured that it was not time. I can tell you that she was thrilled when I told her about going to Greece to investigate my roots."

Sia mostly listened—much of this was news to her. "I had not realized that we have so much in common: Greeks and Turks. It goes against everything I remembered in school. I can tell you, most people I know, even sophisticated types like my father, who worked for a Swedish company and has a master's degree from Canada, would object to the way you characterize our War of Independence."

They stayed until about 11:00 p.m., and then it started to become obvious that Matina was fading, so Yannis and Sia drove Osman to the hotel. They clearly wanted time alone, and to be honest, so did he, with his thoughts.

He got into his Spartan room and kicked off his shoes. The Skype on his phone rang; it was Nilufer.

"Osman, my soul, where have you been? I just get cryptic notes, what is going on?" she screamed, just as the video was coming in.

"I'm sorry, Babe," he said, using the American term she loved to hate.

"OK, then, you are...all right? I thought you were mad at me."
"Why?"
"Cut the crap, Osman. You know why!"
"Because of the Greek thing?" Osman said, almost like a question.
"Yeah, that!"
"Nilufer, I love you; I married all of you, every part. Besides, it looks like we have the 'Greek thing' in common, too."

Nilufer sighed, and whether it was from relief or just exhaustion, she did not know. "I wanted you to know about you before you knew about me. When I found out you had met this Greek who looked like you, I could not believe my good fortune, but I feared the consequences of opening this 'file.'"

Osman stopped for a minute, staring into the small screen on his smartphone. "What 'file'?"

"I mean figuratively. Look, your father knows a lot about his origins and did not tell you. He must have known his people in Antalya had descended from Greek Muslims or Cypriot Muslims. He named you after his father, just as he was named after his grandfather."

"Yes, I guess. What is your point..."

"He had a reason to hide it—to lie about it—and he did not want you to know."

"Maybe," he said, and as he thought about it, he decided that Nilufer was again right.

CHAPTER 11

THE UPPER VILLAGE

Yannis was on time—so un-Greek (or Turkish). It was 10:00 a.m., and from the hotel window he saw Yannis, dressed for the weather, idling over his cell phone in the jeep. Sia was not there.

"Osman, I brought you some heavier jackets and a wool cap and boots," Yannis said, gesturing at the back seat. "The weather is not cooperating, and up five hundred meters or so it can snow, and the temperature will drop at least twelve degrees."

They cleared out of Neapolis in just a few minutes, and soon they were off the small coastal plain, zigzagging up very tight and very steep switchbacks. Osman knew one thing for certain—he would hate negotiating this in the snow, even in a jeep. Reaching a small plateau, they entered the village of Falakro (the bald), which had a Venetian-era fortress in considerable state of ruin overlooking the plain below. In this hideous weather, with rain transforming to flakes while flying vertically, the streets were empty, but the warm light of the one town café caught Yannis's eye, and he stopped abruptly.

"Let's get a coffee…"

The café was full in this awful weather, but very Spartan inside, with rattan chairs and square tables made of either simple wood or round metal with a tablecloth. The television alternated between a sports channel and what looked like a news channel, with multiple talking heads interrupting one another. At seeing Osman walking next to Yannis, everyone did a doubletake; one fellow looked down at his drink to see if he had had more than he should and was seeing double.

Osman was introduced, and everyone, down to the ninety-year-old at his deferential corner table, stood up to shake his hand. Barba Yorgi was his name, and he insisted that Osman sit with him for a drink, though the time was 11:00 a.m. Yannis translated: "Young man, you are our seed; your face speaks of this land, of these mountains. The fates took you across the Aegean, and you forgot your home."

Barba Yorgi wiped a tear, whether for this story or for one of his own. "No matter, you found your way back. My brother, he went to Chile, to some town called Anofagasta or Antofagasta. He forgot his land, and his children and grandchildren—they have never come back."

"You don't know, Barba Yorgi," Yannis offered. "Perhaps his grandchildren or great grandchildren will find their way back here."

Knocking back his tsipouro, Barba Yorgi asked, "And where do you take our nephew?"

"To the Upper Village, Barba Yorgi; his ancestor was probably born there. We had a common great-great-great-grandfather, probably."

"Of course," Barba Yorgi said. "Now I see it. He is from Papou Omer's line: the bey of the Upper Village. A good man: cut down at the massacre of Monemvasia."

As Yannis translated, Osman marveled at the old man's mind and his command of local stories. "Are these legends, *Efendim?*" Osman asked, using the Turkish word of high deference that did not need to be translated.

"Thank you for your words of honor, young man!" Barba Yorgi said. "These are true stories. Two hundred years ago in our mountains, some of our family turned Turk, but remained our people in their hearts. It was a distinction without substance…until it became a reason to kill one another."

"The Revolution."

"Yes, the Maniots and Kalamatans came from across the Laconian Gulf, impressed all Christians into their armies, and slaughtered the few Muslims who fell into their hands, in spite of speaking the same language and having the same blood and traditions."

Here, Barba Yorgi stopped for a moment and called out for the proprietor. "Thanassi, more tsipouro, you cheap bastard!"

Everyone laughed, Barba Yorgi the loudest. "Where was I? OK, so you go out to kill your neighbor, who you have seen every day. Maybe you owe him money, too. Then you get a double benefit: you kill for your faith and for your pocket!"

Here, Osman added, "I read a story that the first person you kill when there is ethnic warfare is the fellow you owe money to."

"Of course!" Barba Yorgi agreed. "You should have seen how it was during our Civil War here. I fought in the mountains across the gulf—in the Tayegetos. Drafted again after serving in the army in Albania in World War Two. Fought under a sadistic captain from Patras, who during the war fought in the German security battalions. Shot my own cousin through the heart, on orders from him. Blew the legs off of an *antartina*, a female guerilla, probably fifteen years old, with the face of an angel and red hair." He shed more tears. "Every time I see a girl with red hair, I break down and cry. Thank God here in Greece red hair is uncommon!" The tears flowed uncontrollably.

"We have tired you, Barba Yorgi," Yannis said, trying to get up.

"Stay, Boy! I am not finished!" he said in a tone that gave no alternative. "I just went down memory lane."

The old man continued, "So, the killing has started, and your ancestor in the Upper Village, the richest man in the village, decides it is best to go to Monemvasia, which for centuries has had the best fortress in the area."

"OK," Yannis interrupted, "but how did his ancestor get to Turkey?"

Osman asked what Yannis said, then offered his own thought. "Maybe my ancestor was one of Omer Bey's sons, who escaped by ship before the siege of Monemvasia began."

Yannis nodded, telling Osman, "Yes, we already discussed this, but I want Barba Yorgi's thoughts."

Barba Yorgi pulled again on his tsipouro and thought for a minute. "By ship, I guess."

"Exactly," Osman said, "I just have to find more proof."

"My son, the proof is here, on your face! You are the brother of Yannis, so many times removed. Fate has joined what politics and war have pulled apart!" He held both of their hands, "Boys, you must never leave each other again; you must be family!"

They looked at each other, and both had tears in their eyes. "Take him to the village, to take some soil from his land. Bless you, and may your children live for you, my nephew Osman! Do you have a son, my boy?"

"Yes," Osman said, tears running down his cheeks. "His name is... Omer, which was my father's name!"

"You see, you see! You followed the tradition of the Greeks: naming your first-born son after your father! That is the proof!"

Kissing Osman on both cheeks, no eyes were dry, and a slightly overwhelmed Osman and Yannis returned to the jeep. The freezing rain had stopped, making the route much easier. More tight switchbacks brought them to the Lower Village, which they drove through quickly, reaching the Upper Village just thirty minutes after leaving the embrace of the café in Falakros.

Patches of snow were everywhere, and the village, consisting of one paved road and a half dozen inhabited houses, was less than Osman had expected. Above and below the main road, other, ruined houses and buildings cluttered the landscape, but clearly the village had never supported more than a few hundred people.

"This boy; he is one of us," Thia Matina (another one) exclaimed. "Our *soi*!" The word, meaning family or kin, did not need to be translated; it was also used in Turkey. A tear ran down Osman's cheek. He produced some boxes of Turkish delight for the villagers: all five of them, all over seventy and representing half the permanent residents of the Upper Village.

Her husband, Barba Christos, poured small glasses of homemade tsipouro for everyone, gathered as they were in a large room with an oversized, antique samovar that also had Turkish coffee brewing. Christos had spent seven years in Australia and a couple of years in Florida "illegally working in restaurants, you know, cash cash cash buziyness" so he could speak enough English to be understood. This was good for Yannis, who became exhausted from constant translation of emotionally heavy subjects.

The septuagenarians asked Osman about his family and children, adding that "may they live for you," a Greek benediction whenever children are mentioned. Looking at the two of them together—Yannis and Osman—Christos said, "You two are more than brothers; you are cut from the same cloth, the cloth of these mountains!"

Barba Haralambos said, "It's true, the green eyes, the shape of the head, you see it everywhere here and everywhere our people went. We are scattered to the four winds like seeds!" he laughed. "But, my child, we are good seeds here."

The conversation turned—like all of his conversations since, well, meeting his twin—back to the events of the 1821 revolution. Osman remembered Thia Matina's point: "Oral histories are more accurate because they are unofficial."

"Tell me about the family."

"Our family," Barba Christos said, pointing at himself and then Osman.

"Yes, Uncle, our family!'

"There are thousands of years of history in this place, my child. But let's talk about the last two or three hundred years, OK?"

"Yes, Uncle."

"Well, the hardiest people always lived here in the Upper Village, and also people who, for one reason or another, wanted either to live free of authority or because they had to flee authority. Many of our line came from Crete after it fell to the Turks."

"When did Crete fall to the Turks?" Osman asked.

"Oh, around 1650 or so, I am not sure, but these lands here were poor and mountainous, and many Cretans came here. Soon Venice took the whole Morea, the Peloponnesus, from the Ottomans, but held it for only a few years—like twenty or so. Some people became rich, but Venice made them pay big taxes. Venice got thrown out of the Morea in I think 1715, just about one hundred years before our revolution against the Turks."

"Yes, I heard that. I spoke to several historians about this period—Greeks and Turks—and I also consulted sources in the English language, primarily British historians," Osman said as Yannis laboriously translated. "So I know about the Venetian era and the revolution." Trying to be delicate, he added, "Most sources simply write that the Muslims were massacred. I recently found out that some escaped, primarily to Antalya."

"I did not know that there were Turks, I mean, Muslims, who escaped," Barba Christos said. "I thought that some people, like our ancestors, converted."

"Apparently, before the siege was joined by the fleets of Hydra and Spetses, some Turkish supply ships left Monemvasia with refugees who settled in Antalya and a couple of other villages on the Aegean coast of Turkey." He stopped for a moment before adding, "My father, he was from Antalya, and his roots there went back well over one hundred years..."

Interrupting Osman, Barba Christos said, "Son, you are one of us. I don't need to know where your father is from to prove that you are one of us." Drumming his chest loudly, he said, "It's what is in here, boy; your heart is from the Vatika.[22] Your face is your witness, and the rest is just, well, to prove it in the history books."

"You know this, Osman, my nephew, and Yanni, you also know it. Man and his politics and his killing in the name of God had pulled us apart, but God, acting in His mighty name, put us back together."

"Do you really think?" Yannis asked, incredulous.

"Why did you go to Smyrna, Yanni? You were never interested in history. Most of us know these stories. For you it was sports, women, and work. What made you to go there?"

"You know, a friend of mine in Athens—an army buddy—had paid for the tickets for him and his girlfriend. She dumped him, and he was out the money and offered me the ticket for half," Yannis said matter-of-factly. "But if I am totally honest, something really pushed me to go. I had enough going on in my life—my divorce, my daughter, my new girlfriend, my possible move to Australia—but something told me I just had to go."

He reached over to Osman and grasped his hand. "Meeting you has opened my mind to just how connected we all are."

"God wants wrongs to be righted—sometimes it takes generations, sometimes centuries. The circle is always closed; this is the mathematics of the universe," Barba Christo said, smiling.

---

22 The region of the Peloponnesian Peninsula where Neapolis and the Upper Village are located.

Outside, the wind howled, and when the rain changed to snow, it came down hard. Looking outside, Yannis shook his head. "Nothing doing on going back tonight. The roads will be ice. We will have to bunk here."

"Of course you will; Osman must sleep in his ancestors' village. This is your home, now. You are one of us, and you found your way home."

In an upper room warmed by the samovar, a bed was prepared. "My child, this is your room whenever you come here, and when you bring your family," Thia Matina exclaimed, kissing him and taking her leave.

The two "brothers" slept on opposite beds in the room, talking as if they were little boys, both giddy and giggling. "Yannis, aside from the birth of my children, no day has given me more pleasure than today. I feel I am reborn. And I know who I am, finally."

"You are complete. You are more complicated. I am happy with the complications in life; all I want is to make enough money to live a decent life. I am your twin, but, how do you say, your opposite, no?"

"What are you going to do?"

"I don't know. I have a daughter, and there is simply no work here. I have a new person in my life, but she is younger and wants (maybe) different things. I just want to get paid and have my week-ends for football and maybe a cookout with friends or some time at the beach. I am forty, and I have less money—and less chance to make money—than I did when I was twenty," Yannis said, rubbing his eyes with fatigue.

"Then you will go to Australia, and I will never see you," Osman said, suddenly really sad at the prospect.

"Osman, you did without me before, and you will again. I am sorry to be so, you know, hard, but this is the truth. I didn't need to find myself—you do." He saw this hurt Osman. "I am glad I know the truth about my history and our connection to each other, but it will not pay my bills."

"But Yannis, isn't it wonderful that we found each other?"

"Osman, I do not mean to hurt you, but there is something you should know. I had a brother, or someone closer than a brother. His name is Panos."

"What happened to him? Did he, um, die?"

"He is my cousin, he is alive, but I am dead to him," Yannis said, uncharacteristically emotional. "And do you want to know why? Because I took you in my home!"

"Come on, nobody is that bigoted. Everyone I met here has welcomed me."

"Everyone here did not lose their father in Cyprus; he did. My uncle was killed in your invasion of Cyprus. He grew up alone; we both went to the Special Forces, where he had served to honor him. My cousin still serves in the Special Forces; he is a marine sergeant."

In spite of the warm woodburning stove, the air went chill. Osman felt an ominous pallor descending on him. Not noticing, Yannis continued. "When I told him that I had a Turkish 'twin,' and that you wanted to visit, he nearly hit me, and told me that I was never welcome in his house again." Yannis's voice cracked. "This man has been my playmate from birth; he lived with us as much as with his widowed mother. He was the brother I never had, and now he is gone."

Osman felt a tightness in his neck: a sure sign of both stress and a feeling he often got that his good intentions were actually becoming a road to Hell. "My wife warned me about this."

"I am glad I found you, Osman, but you cannot replace what I lost. You are a good man, and a deep one. Much smarter than me, I can see, but you search for answers that will rip people apart. You will suffer, too, I just don't know how." Yawning, Yannis said, "There, that is enough; shut down the light, we must go as soon as the sun melts the ice in the morning."

The old people were up early, cooking up omelets for "the boys," who came downstairs, eagerly accepting the Greek coffee as soon as it brimmed up in its small copper pot. The fire had gone out in the evening, and it was bitter cold, though perhaps it was Osman's sense of foreboding that chilled him so much. While demanding that they stay further, Osman, thinking of Yannis, said, "I need to leave for Athens tomorrow, and the next morning, to Smyrna."

Translating this, Yannis nodded in agreement. No eyes were dry, least of all Osman's, who now felt heavy in spite of the euphoria of the past few days. As they pulled out of the village, the Rock of Monemvasia gleamed in the morning air; the bright sun painted the rock with dazzling hues. "Our ancestors must have seen this many times, and my ancestor might have remembered the Rock as his last memory of his home," Osman said.

"Yes, I never tire of this view. I have seen it a thousand times." Having idled the car to take in the view, he put the gear in first and started off. "Osman, I was unfair to you last night. I feel lost and cut off from my roots, and you think you found your roots. I can see I hurt you."

"No, brother, you did not. Something else hurts me. You spoke of your uncle who was killed in Cyprus. My father was there, a young lieutenant, in the heat of the fight."

"I see, well what can be done about that? It was war, and he was a soldier. I was a soldier for three years. Shit happens, Osman."

Going down was much faster than coming up, and Yannis drove with speed and confidence. These were his mountains, and he knew every turn in every weather. Osman just watched, and every scene he saw from the eyes of his refugee ancestor. He felt that he, too, was now going into exile, back to his father's apartment house, where the history was official and patriotic, and the Cyprus invasion was heroic, just, and honorable. That felt like exile, and he quite frankly didn't think he could do that again.

Not that Nilufer wanted to; she had been holding her history secret from Osman, waiting for Osman to be ready to accept how life and origins were, by necessity, complicated. They had been talking about moving abroad, perhaps to Canada. He had been quietly sending out inquiries. But now, with both of them "out," how do you go back into the cage?

He didn't know, and as Yannis gunned the Jeep down the serpentine road, his whole life unfolded in front of him. His father: always in uniform, always guarded in his actions and his history, but too loudly Turkish and nationalistic. And Osman: the bookish, sensitive son who was drawn to the West and to literature dissecting complicated characters and histories—stories discouraged in his own country. Nilufer: the quiet city girl with a busy smile, who was hiding a secret identity in plain sight, and who loved him in spite of his complexes. Now, he uncovered his family's—his Turkish father's—secret Greek history. He was both thrilled yet utterly anxious, as if the euphoria he presently felt would soon be shattered.

Did my father know? Osman was certain he did. It explained his peacock nationalism, his insistence on following Turkish state mythology slavishly. Yet he kept traditions "of his family" that pointed to an obvious Greek origin. Was that why he hated Greeks so much?

Or was it something else? And why was Yannis the one who could answer the question?

"My cousin, Panos, sent me a letter, a package actually. I do not know what was in it. I did not want to open it."

Now, in spite of the cold, Osman felt his shirt moist with sweat. "Did you, a, open it?"

"No, I couldn't. I don't want to see what's inside. Probably some propaganda, or something to make me feel bad."

They arrived at Yannis's apartment. Sia called out to them from the balcony. "Hello, my twins, how was the trip to the Upper Village?"

Pulling small packs out of the back seat, the two men went in, Yannis happy to see his mate, but Osman visibly tense.

"What is it, Osman?" Sia asked, "You look very uncomfortable."

"Nothing, I am just overwhelmed by everything."

Sia nodded, her smile suddenly becoming a frown. "Well, something disturbing happened this morning. I saw an envelope with no name—probably from some Golden Dawn member because Osman is here. It was a picture from the Cyprus invasion. I opened it, absently. I'm really sorry I did."

Yannis took the picture, nodding in recognition. "I did not open it. It's very upsetting, I would imagine."

A grainy black-and-white photo, obviously taken in haste and in secret, showed several Greek commandos on their knees in surrender, guarded by grinning Turkish soldiers. Next to the kneeling prisoners, two are sprawled out, shot through the head. In spite of the shadow, one of the commandos' faces is clearly visible, his piercing eyes transfixed in a mixture of fear, rage, and defiance: Yannis's uncle Haralambos, Panos's father.

Yannis regretted that Sia showed this picture while Osman was here, but Osman took it from his hands and started trembling.

"My God, now I know...everything!"

In the picture there was a Turkish junior officer, sufficiently swaggering and wearing sunglasses against the hot Cypriot sun. Closer to the photographer, his face was clearly visible, as was the pistol he ever so recently used.

"This is...my father!"

Yannis looked at Osman, at once so sad and so angry. "*He* did this? To prisoners! Is this what you people do?"

"I knew; somehow I knew. I am so sorry; how can I make amends?"

"There is nothing you can do. But you must leave!" Stuttering with rage, he said in Greek, "Sia, take him to the hotel, I cannot."

Sia wanted to object, but this was not the time. She picked up Osman's bag and led a stunned Osman out of the house.

"Sia, I knew, deep in my heart. I knew…"

"Osman, Yannis is a dear man; he is just in shock. How can a mystery twin replace everything he has known? I don't want to sound, as the British say, 'posh,' but Yannis is not a thinker; he is just a doer. For you, it is a journey of discovery; for him, finding this out just, how can I say, validates his cousin's hatred toward you."

"I understand him; I am just saying that I knew that my father did something terrible in Cyprus—something he could not forgive himself for doing—and that's why he always screamed about the Greeks. He was in a sort of pain."

Sia nodded, and he continued. "I think it hurt all the more for him to know that he had Greek blood. He must have known, because he would get so angry if I suggested it. And my wife is from a Crypto-Christian mother. Like the Facebook status, 'it's complicated'!"

They were outside the hotel. Sia kissed him on both cheeks and tried to make a joke. "This time, my kiss is more chaste than when we met!" She laughed nervously and sadly.

"Take care of my brother; send him my love and my eternal thanks. I will…miss him," he said dejectedly.

Suddenly, Sia stiffened, as if reading Osman's thoughts. "Osman, you are, um, going to drive back to Athens tonight?"

"Why do you ask?"

"I think you know why! Don't bullshit with me! You can do that with Yannis; he is straightforward and you have a language barrier. I speak perfect English like you, and I also, if you forgive me, feel you. Somehow I think your wife is a lot like me."

"It's true, Sia," Osman said. "You could be cousins."

"We just might be. I had a grandmother from Smyrna, but that is another story for another day. Listen carefully: if you are thinking to make things right, as it were, with Panos, forget it and get in your car now! Panos is blinded by his pain and will not hesitate to kill you. He has spent twelve years in the Special Forces and could break your neck in a flash! Do you understand? If I have to, I will pack you myself and drive you to Athens!"

"OK, I understand. I have a wife and children, you know."

"Yes, I do, and he does not. He has nothing to lose, and he has endured this pain for decades; don't open this Pandora's Box!"

"OK, I got it."

Back in his room, Osman set down his backpack and wept, whether from the emotion of the last two weeks of self-discovery or from the latest revelation, which he somehow always knew, he could not say. He thought to call Nilufer, but how? Hearing her voice would stop him from what he had to do. He knew it, Sia knew it, and there would be no stopping him.

CHAPTER 12

ATONEMENT FOR THE SINS OF THE FATHER

"I'm going to that café, and I will find Panos!"

He ran by reception without a word, but Sia, suspecting what he would do, asked them to call her immediately. He went to Billinis's Café, where everyone greeted him initially as Yannis but then remembered that "a Turk" had been visiting Yannis who looked just like him. "I am looking for Panos, please," Osman said, trembling just a bit.

In the corner a muscular, swarthy fellow with a thick leather jacket rose to his feet. *He looks like the Pomak*[23] *ex-mob guy who ran security for Husayn! Oh, God.*

"What you want?" Panos said, in obviously broken English.

"I want to talk to you, Panos. Can we speak privately?"

"What is privately?"

A fellow next to him told him. "OK, outside."

A couple of his friends followed them out. Panos told them to stay back.

"Speak, Turk, and make it quick. I don't like you."

Trembling, "Sir, I came here to find my origins. Your great-great-great-great-grandfather and Yannis's were the same person."

"Eh, Pavlo, what is this *malaka*[24] saying?"

---

23 Pomak is a Bulgarian speaking Muslim subethnicity that lives in Bulgaria and Greece. Many have immigrated to Turkey, particularly those from Bulgaria.

24 Malaka is the Greek equivalent of the British English term "wanker."

Pavlos translated.

"So who gives a fuck?"

"During your revolution most Muslims were killed, but my ancestor escaped; yours converted to Christianity. Both of our fathers fought in Cyprus."

Panos's eyes, which were the same shade of green as Osman's, narrowed. "So, your father was in Cyprus? In war?"

Trembling even more, Osman said, "I saw the picture…" He did not need to finish the story. A giant fist hit him in the face. As he fell back, a feminine voice screamed, "No!"

Sia had followed him here, losing Osman just for a minute while she called Yannis. "Get your ass down to the café; Osman is going to tell Panos. Move your ass!"

Sia jumped between Osman and Panos. Osman got to his feet. "Panos, I came to apologize; I thought you needed to know that I am sorry for what he did!"

Panos shoved Sia aside and again floored Osman, who managed to get to his knees. "I am on my knees. I have kids. I am sorry. Please forgive me, I had to ask for forgiveness!"

Sia, seeing that he did not understand, translated, and added, "Panos, he is offering to trade his life; he feels responsible. But if you kill him, you are the same as his father!"

"Bitch, shut up, before I…"

"Before you what, Pano?" Yannis screamed. "Back away from both of them, now!"

Osman put his hands in the air, tears of pain, fear, and regret streaming down his face. "My father is a killer, I knew it; I needed to prove it. If you want to be like him, then kill me."

"Kill me, too, Pano!" Yannis screamed as he stood in front of Osman. "You won't heal by spilling blood. This man came here to learn about his secrets. We are the same blood, literally, and his father spilled it. We spilled it in the past, too."

Sia stood in front of Yannis. "End it here, Pano! Stop the spilling of blood in the family. It's in your power!"

Fists clenched in rage, Panos burst into tears and slowly backed away. Nobody said anything; they just waited. When Panos backed away enough and his countenance changed, Osman said softly, "Please ask him for forgiveness, and thank him for sparing my life."

The crowd dispersed, and the sun had already set over the Maniot Mountains to the west. Panos's crew took the shaking, crying man into Billinis's Café, alternatively cursing the Turk and praising Panos's humanity. Given the era we are in, it all got caught on iPhone. One of the spectators was an unemployed freelance writer from Athens who was down in Neapolis visiting a girlfriend.

Yannis put Osman in Sia's care and instructed her to drive with him back to Athens in Osman's rented car—tonight. There was no guarantee that Panos might regret his kindness and come after Osman again. Poor Panos was a long-wounded soul, but he was also a local personality, and he might get goaded by some of the local toughs to finish the job. Yannis thought it best to let Panos cool off before he approached him, and that could take a while.

Maybe this was the jolt he needed to go to Australia, at least for a few months. Sia was ready to go, and his daughter, Maria, could go with them for the summer vacation. His ex-wife, Soula, was ready to accept this, and his uncle's restaurant in Melbourne had plenty of work for Yannis and Sia. It was not ideal, but these were the times. Yannis knew that he was lucky to have an uncle in Melbourne with a restaurant, with no kids, and with a great fondness for him. His friend Haralambos continued to remind him of this.

It was time to go, for a while at least...

Sia gunned the car toward Sparta. The road was, well, a bit irregular until then, and after climbing Parnon Mountain, the superhighway began. From Tripolis to Athens was ninety minutes with Sia behind the wheel. She didn't say much, at least until Sparta.

Climbing up Parnon, at the summit, she pulled over to a taverna. "Can we eat or at least have a meze? I'm hungry and just weirded out."

"Yes, of course, Sia."

They walked into the roadside taverna with a roasted lamb and pig on a spit outside. "I need some wine," Osman said. "I am shaking inside."

"I'll bet you are; so am I!" Sia said. "I just knew you would confront Panos. You cannot undo things; you cannot make things right that were wrong."

She saw that Osman was hurt, so she continued more gently, "You know, Osman, you had a lot of courage, what you did. You put your head on the block. I admire you."

"Don't. I had to do it. My father has carried this guilt all of his life, and I knew he carried this guilt. I did it for him; I did it for me. I had a good life because he was an officer, and in his first battle, he freaked out and went from being a hero to a murderer." Taking a long drink, he sighed. "Deep down, he never forgave himself, and he needed a lifetime to justify it." He stopped, and downed the house white wine served in a small glass typical of Greek rural tavernas.

Osman grinned slightly. "He knew about the Greek connection—not just from here, but he had Cypriot blood, too. He knew all of it, and he was embarrassed; he felt he wasn't Turkish enough, and at the same time he must have felt that, somehow, like he was killing his own in Cyprus."

Sia drank her own glass. "I don't know; I did not know any of this. My own life was pretty sheltered: I lived in a nice suburb of Athens. I had a summer home on the beach, a dad with a good job, and like every Greek kid I was friends with, a master's degree abroad—in my case in Leeds, in Britain."

Osman listened. Sia threw back her frizzy black hair. "I had a grandmother born in Smyrna, I mean, Izmir; she came to Salonika as a little girl. The rest of my family is from Macedonia or the island of Corfu. I was never interested in history, just partying on the beach or shopping. In England, most of my friends were other Greeks. There were a few Italians, but really no British people. There were some Turkish students. We were nice to one another, but we were very, how do you say, cliquish."

"What has changed? You would not be telling me this if something had not changed."

She nodded. "I think it was meeting Yannis, and the possibility that we will leave for Australia. We pretty much decided on it, and I think that, after today, it is a good idea to get out of town for a while." She poured both of them more wine from the cylindrical copper tin, nodding to the waiter for more. "Actually, it was you, too. Meeting you."

Osman smiled. "Why me?"

"Because I have learned from you that so much of our history that we learned is really just politics, not history. Mythology really. I used to think that Greece and Greeks had figured everything out. We had the best culture, the smartest people, and a history that went back to the glories of Ancient Greece."

"It is a nice story to grow up with."

"We blamed you for everything. We knew that, deep down, we are backward and primitive, and we said, 'It's because of the Turks.'" Throwing out a finger in mock accusation, she said, "You did this to us!"

Seeing Osman flinch, still in shock from the day's events, she immediately took his hand kindly. "Sorry Osman—too soon for humor, eh?"

"Yes," Osman said flatly.

"I'm sorry, it was insensitive and particularly with what happened today."

"We are two sides of the same coin. And both Greeks and Turks are good and bad, or good or bad." Tears started to flow.

"I upset you; I am so sorry!" She got out of her chair to hug Osman.

"It's for my father. How can I ever embrace him again, knowing what I know? My son is named after him, Greek-style, just like I was named after his father."

"Osman, where are you going to stay in Athens? I can put you up if you want."

"No, I think I will call my wife's friend, Ebru; she is a Turkish lady who works for a Turkish bank here in Athens." He fiddled for his cell phone, and then dialed her.

"Ebru, it's Osman here."

"Osman, I have been wondering how your journey to your roots has been going. You are still in Greece, right?"

"Yes, I am on my way back to Athens, a..."

"...did you have a good time?" she asked, hearing the stress in his voice.

"Ebru, I had the best and the worst time. I found my history, my roots, and I found out some more recent, more disturbing history."

Ebru was suddenly worried, "Are you hurt? What happened? Do you need help? Does Nilufer know?"

"Would you shut up and let me talk, Ebru?"

"OK, what happened?"

"Well, you know my double, Yannis? We are related. I learned the story when I went to the village; it has to be true. My father knew it. I have new family," Osman blurted out.

"Well, that is good, right?" Ebru interrupted. "So, what is the problem?"

"Well, Yannis has a cousin; his name is Panos. He lost his father in Cyprus. My, my father, killed him!"

"What? How do you know? This is ridiculous! Just because they both fought in Cyprus does not make your father his killer!"

"It does when you saw a smuggled picture of your father shooting Greek prisoners including his father!"

"Oh my God! Osman, I am so sorry—this is terrible! How you must feel!"

"I feel an open pain, but I always, deep down, knew that he did something—there, specifically—that he could not forgive himself for doing. He also had to have known he had some Greek ancestry. He knew too much history not to know. He hid behind his uniform and our flag."

"Everyone hides behind something, and the flag is a typical veil, more so than the feredje so many of our women—but not Nilufer or I—wear!"

"Yes, but I could not hide. I went to the cousin, Panos, and I told him. He is a commando; he hit me a few times and would have killed me except for Yannis and especially Yannis's girlfriend, Sia. She is here with me now, driving me back to Athens."

"Osman, I feared that you would learn too much, I just knew it. I think you did, too."

"I did."

"You showed exceptional courage to reveal yourself to this Panos guy. You met him on his home ground." She breathed deeply. "Are you hurt, I mean physically hurt?"

"A bit bruised. I thought my jaw was broken, but I am OK."

"How can I help, Osman?"

"Can I come to your house, to stay there tonight and maybe to-morrow? I have an open ticket for the flight home to Izmir."

"You know you can. Shall I call Nilufer?"

"Yes, that would be a good idea. Right now, I…I cannot talk to her. I am too shredded."

While Sia and Osman were on their way back to Athens, Angela Dimitriou was at her friend's house, furiously typing away at her lap-top. She contacted Stavros Thomopoulos, an editor of an Athenian tabloid she sometimes worked with, about a "Human Interest Story with International Implications."

Two hours later, just as Sia and Osman were entering Athens's Ring Motorway, Angela uploaded her story, a video, and selected still pictures to Stavros.

Angela's phone rang almost immediately. "Dimitriou, this is good! You got it; I want to publish this. I will remit two hundred euros to your account. We get all publishing rights." Stopping for a second to reread he added, "Really this is great!"

Sia wound through the quiet streets of midnight Athens to Ebru's apartment in Pangrati. Luckily, they were able to find parking nearby, and Osman pulled his suitcase out of the trunk. Sia was getting ready to take her leave, but Osman held her hand hard. "Don't leave! Please, I am too stressed and Ebru will have tons of questions." Looking intently into her eyes, he pleaded, "I can't do it alone."

Ebru met them at the door, embracing Osman carefully so that she wouldn't hurt him. "Osman, you crazy brave boy! Let's get you cleaned up." She handed the key to Sia. "It's on the second floor," she said, and went out to a nearby all-night pharmacy, sizing up his needs with a couple of looks. "Are you hurt anywhere else?"

"No."

Ebru cleaned, disinfected, and bandaged Osman's cuts while Sia told Ebru everything that had happened, and also a bit more about Panos. "I am sorry for him, too, and it took a fair amount of courage for him not to finish the job in the presence of so many of his gang."

"That's why Yannis is coming up here tomorrow. We'll make arrangements for Australia. We're done with here."

Ebru prepared a small Greek salad, opened a can of sardines, and led them to the table. "Look at us," Ebru said. "We are meant to be sitting at the same table, but instead we are divided by politics and religion. Our countries took the table away from us—only we should have the right to choose who sits at our table." Ebru then tossed her head back. "Fuck these states!"

Sia took this in. Until recently, she had no problem with Greece and being Greek. She loved the way of life, and Greece was a country that, she felt, had figured it out. They lived well, the chaos was manageable if you were used to it and if you had enough money and connections, and though she cared little for it, the history and culture of Greece was admired around the world.

In Britain she had several professors who were wide-eyed philhellenes, combining a love of the classics with more earthly and earthy experiences during their Greek summer holidays to become devoted to and advocates for the large Greek student population at her Mildlands university. One such professor—a scholarly, brooding fifty-year-old—left his wife for a raven-haired, voluptuous fellow student of Sia's. Upon graduation, she promptly dumped her would-be Lord Byron and decamped to Crete, warning him in no uncertain terms that if he followed her or if he revealed the relationship to her relatives, he might end up on the working end of a Kalashnikov.

Though she secretly felt sorry for the professor, at the time, like all of the Greek students, she mocked him, almost to his face. She was not above reaping dividends for being from the "Cradle of Democracy and Western Civilization," but there were limits. She went out a few times with a Classics student—a wealthy and bookish boy from Devon—but she never went much beyond the platonic, lying through her teeth that "nice Greek girls don't do that."

To the degree that she cared, she liked the deference some Brits showed the Greeks due to the beautiful holidays they spent there and the shadow still cast by ancient Greek civilization. Also, though the British government generally supported Turkey, individual Brits still looked on Turks as somehow barbaric.

And here she was, in a poor but hip and edgy part of Athens, in a Turkish woman's apartment, with a Turkish man who looked the spitting, but more bookish, image, of her boyfriend. That resemblance, moreover, was not accidental; there was enough evidence to show that Yannis and Osman were in fact related by blood. Then there was the blond Ebru, who looked like a Bosnian because, in fact, she was a Bosnian. Ebru and Osman told her about Osman's wife, Nilufer, and her Greek roots.

"It's complicated...to say the least."

Or is it? Sia wondered. *Did we make it complicated? By making hermetically sealed identities, set up in opposition to one another, have we made things complicated? Do we need to feed bodies to war, to keep the walls up?*

She put these questions to Ebru, who just shook her head. "An old man, a Serbian cameraman in Sarajevo, told me, 'There is no worse species in the animal kingdom than the human.' He was right." Pulling on her filterless cigarette, she added, "However, I have seen the kindness of strangers and the table of fellowship work miracles."

"After the past day or two, I am more convinced than ever that we need to move to Australia," Sia said. "I resisted it before, but I just want to get away to a place with many nationalities and the chance to earn a living."

Ebru's slightly lined and wise face smiled. "Sia, don't expect miracles there, either. I meet plenty of Greek Australians here in Greece; they are often more nationalistic than Greeks here. In Bosnia, there were plenty of Serb Australian paramilitaries. The ethnic communities are very strong there."

"I understand, and Yannis's uncle is a fixture in the local Greek community with a strong business there, but I don't care. I just want to earn money and to hopefully start a family with Yannis. I want a clean slate—no more Greek myths."

"Don't forget Australian myths..." Ebru cautioned. "And remember, you will always be part of here. You cannot just transition from one sealed identity to the other. If you learn anything from Osman's story, learn that."

"I understand, but I have lived in Britain, which created Australia. Even though I was just a typical Greek student there, there was the chance to be myself. British people respect your individuality. Not like Greeks..."

"...or Turks, believe me."

"I do. After everything I have learned the past few days, I see that we are not that different; we are two sides of the same coin."

The spring sun began to rise over Hymnettus Mountain. It was 6:00 a.m. Poor Osman was snoring in Ebru's bedroom, as Ebru rolled another cigarette while the Turkish coffee brewed on the stove. Sia watched the small pot to stop it from overflowing.

On the other side of the Aegean, Nilufer was awake and putting the last items in her bag. The kids had stayed at her cousin's house, and the cab to the airport would be here in twenty minutes. The plane for Athens would leave at 9:30.

Ebru took a cursory glance at her e-mail. She received daily updates from a half-dozen Greek, English, and Turkish language online newspapers. *Live Athens*, an Athenian online and print magazine, was always on her "to-scan" list. Thumbing through the articles, she froze:

Shocker: Sins of Turkish Father in Cyprus Invasion Almost Visited Upon the Son!
By Angela Dimitriou
NEAPOLIS—Last night, wounds from the Cyprus Invasion of 1974 were reopened. A Turkish tourist, Osman Celik, having learned that his father may have been the executioner—murderer in fact—of a martyred Greek hero from the conflict confronted the martyr's son, Panos Kontos. The son, a decorated member of our Special Forces, naturally took his decades-old sorrow out on the Turkish tourist, but was persuaded by his relatives and by his own sense of humanity to spare him. This act of mercy is something that should make us all proud.

Apparently, Osman Celik, son of retired Turkish colonel Omer Celik, works for a large Turkish textile concern with interests in investing in our country. He was in Neapolis to investigate whether his paternal ancestors were in fact Greek Muslims from the Neapolis district. Assisting him was a local Greek, Yannis Meimetis: a cousin of Panos Kontos's who is said to be the "identical twin" of Osman Celik, prompting both men to investigate their origins.

A few minutes later, all the phones began a cacophony. Sia got a call from Yannis, besieged for more than two hours by reporters, and now Ebru's phone rang, with a pointed call from her boss as to "what she knew about Celik's activities in Neapolis." The article had just appeared in English on the *Live Athens* English page, and Diaspora Greek media were posting the link as well.

HaberIzmirWeb, a Turkish online portal from Izmir, also posted the link in English. The human and international interest of this story was reaching critical mass in this digital viral age. Nilufer's phone rang before she boarded for Athens, with HaberIzmirWeb asking for her take on the article. Taken aback, she hung up, grateful to be on a plane for an hour and away from the shrill ring of the cell phone and the piling text messages. Twenty had arrived by the time she had to turn off her cell phone.

Omer Celik had not heard his daughter-in-law leave. He was up at 7:00 a.m.—a bit later than usual—but just as he returned from the bathroom, his landline rang. *The nerve of people calling me at this hour!* "Celik speaking!"

"Colonel Celik?"

"The same. Who are you, and how do you have the impudence to call at such an early time?"

"Colonel, Sir, my name is Reha Devlet, feature editor of *HaberIzmirWeb*."

"Never heard of it; are you some kind of newspaper?"

"Yes, Colonel, we publish on the Internet."

"Then you are not a serious newspaper. Good day..."

"Wait, Efendi, please, do you know your son was involved in an altercation in Greece?"

"What happened?" Then, suddenly terrified for his son, he asked, "Is my son OK?"

"Yes, Colonel, there is a small article about what happened. Do you have an Internet connection?"

"Well, yes, I do, but what happened?

"He got into a fight with a Greek over, um, events in Cyprus?"

"What events? What are you talking about?"

"From 1974, from our 'liberation' of Cyprus," the editor offered, using a Turkish characterization of the 1974 invasion.

"You are fencing with me; out with it!"

"I don't know much; it was a two-paragraph article, but it says he got into a fight with the man whose father you killed in Cyprus!"

"I killed a lot of people in Cyprus; it was war. It was either me or them. What happened to my son?" His chest was tightening.

"I do not know yet, Sir; we thought you might be able to explain."

As the editor spoke, however, he did another Internet search. Now there was a picture. Dimitriou had contacted Panos, who provided her with a copy of the picture showing his father's murder, and the midmorning version of the article had both the picture and some input from Panos. It was in English, and it was sent deliberately to Reha to further its publishing in Turkey.

"I don't have to explain anything. I fought for Turkey against the enemy. I am hardly going to defend my actions or those of our army. My son had no business visiting these cursed Greeks. Now, tell me, is he injured?"

Reha barely followed what the colonel had said, skimming instead the article and matching a service photo of Omer with the young officer in sunglasses. After Omer paused, Reha began, "Colonel Celik, Efendi, your son is fine; he cannot be reached for comment, but he left in the company of a young woman, the girlfriend of his host, who apparently looks exactly like your son."

"Oh, yes, he told me he met a Greek tourist that looked exactly like him; it had obsessed him." With an authoritative voice echoing his military past, he said, "This conversation is over!"

"Thank you, Colonel Efendi," Reha said, almost relishing the old man's arrogance. "Perhaps you will care to visit our webpage or this afternoon's newspaper. There is a picture you might like to comment on."

Click.

Colonel Celik felt his stomach tighten in a more acute version of the pain he had felt ever since the Cyprus invasion whenever he was physically or emotionally stressed. He had already had a serious heart attack three years ago. He searched the Internet for facts, but he was not particularly Internet savvy, and his English language skills were very limited. He found *HaberIzmirWeb* and saw the article, together with another article that came up in Greek, but had a...the picture! His fingers shook on the keyboard.

"So this is it, then?" Omer sighed. "My son knows. I hoped he would not know until I . . ." He felt the heaviness grow in his chest, like a tank was on him.

Colonel Celik always knew that the bill would be presented for his act. He could hardly conceive that it would come from his son's chance meeting with a Greek who was both a distant relative of his and a close relative of the man Omer killed. He had to admit that there was an elegance with which the fates had played this one. It was executed with military precision. His chest tightened further. *Should he call for Nilufer?*

He rang the home number, then her cell phone. Both went to voicemail, and the pain continued. Shall he call for an ambulance?

No, he searched further on the Internet. This time, a second article appeared in Turkish that talked about Osman confronting the man whose father Omer had killed, and it specifically referenced the picture. Tears came down Omer's eyes...

"My son, he sought to atone for me..."

The pain in his chest got sharper; if he did not call emergency services, he was done for. Nobody was at the apartment building, and as he struggled to the balcony to shout, he stumbled. He grabbed his phone again, knowing that this was his last chance to tell his son his own story from this side of the grave.

Dialing, the call went to voicemail: "Osman my son. I love you, I know you know everything, and I know that what you did, you did for me. There is a letter locked in my drawer for you. To be opened after..."

The message ended, and he was at his last. Osman would find the letter, and the vision his father saw as he passed out of this life was that of Osman's children rather than the eyes of his victim from four decades ago—the eyes he saw nearly every day.

Hikmet also received e-mail notifications from various newspapers and magazines. He was a packrat for information on others and had keyword searches set up for various people he sought to track, including Osman. "Today, his inbox was full of searches. The article, in English, from *HaberIzmirWeb,* was a treasure trove. It roughly translated the English version of the Athens article into Turkish, adding and subtracting for Turkish sensibilities. "So, our Osman is a secret *Yunan*[25] and he also spits in the face of his hero father!" Hikmet rubbed his hands together with glee. "I am sure Husayn Bey would find this very interesting!"

Or would he? Husayn was not particularly nationalistic, and he despised Kemalist secular types like Colonel Celik. No, the story would have to be presented to Husayn in a manner most damning to Osman.

Nilufer's plane descended quickly into Athens as she looked out anxiously over the Aegean below her. She felt multiple trepidations about this trip. Her secret Greek identity was now out in the open, and Osman had obviously bitten off more than he could chew here.

The Greek immigration official smiled at Nilufer, and welcomed her to Greece in English. His smile widened when she replied to his further questions in a rusty, but steady Greek. She picked up her small suitcase at baggage claim and walked out into the terminal, where a waiting Ebru showered her with kisses.

"Ebru, my dear! Thank you for helping my Osman. Where is he?"

---

25 In Turkish, it literally translates as Ionian, but it is the term Turks use for Greeks from Greece (*Yunanistan*).

"At my apartment. The Greek guy's girlfriend is watching over him. He was full of nervous exhaustion by the time she drove him to Athens. He sacked out and has not woken up."

Nilufer looked at Ebru, sort of scared. "Don't worry, that is why I left him in the Greek girl's care. She is keeping an eye on him." Looking at her small handcarry suitcase, "that is it, right, let's go."

As they made for the exit, a man stopped her and said in English, "Excuse me, are you Nilufer Celik?"

"Yes," she said automatically, though she regretted it, "Who are you?"

"I am a journalist and I wanted to know if you had any comment on…"

"No, she doesn't!" Ebru interjected in Greek. "Now leave her alone." Then, in Turkish to Nilufer, she said, "I was worried about this. Now they will follow us."

She hailed a cab, whose driver luckily had the skills to rid them of their pursuers.

Nilufer ran into Ebru's house and embraced her groggy husband, who was clearly still reeling from yesterday's events. In the space of a few weeks, Osman's life had been turned upside down. It was pointless to talk about it—the look of spouses with a lot of history and love between them told it all. She put her hand to his lips. "Don't speak, my soul; I read your tired and beautiful face."

Tears ran down their faces—all of their faces. Ebru sat them down at the table. "I contacted your cousin in Izmir, to check on the kids." She said, "They are fine, but the story is all over the Internet and the news in Izmir."

Osman's face shot up. "They must have contacted my father! Oh no!"

He fumbled for his mobile phone; where there were more than one hundred messages. His mailbox was full, but he saw his father's number and called it. No answer. He tried again, and then checked his voicemails, skipping all of them until it reached his father's number, where a heavily wheezing Omer Celik recorded his last words.

Osman dropped the phone, "It is finished; he is gone. He asked for forgiveness and blessed me!"

Here Osman's knees gave out, and as he fainted, Sia caught him as he was going down, softening a fall that may have caused a serious injury. Nilufer screamed, but the sharp-witted Ebru pulled out some smelling salts—why she had such things, only Merciful Allah knows.

EPILOGUE: ONE YEAR LATER

Osman got out of his car, doubling his scarf against the cold. A vicious wind whipped off of Lake Ontario, and he yet again forgot his gloves. A five-minute walk from the parking lot to the office was excruciating in this wind, but the idea of wearing gloves, particularly when it should be springtime, was hard to bear.

He threw his laptop case over his shoulder and struggled against a headwind. The sun was up, thank God, as the winter darkness had maddened them, and change to daylight savings time was a blessing in spite of getting up early.

The children have adapted well, at least... Osman reminded himself, smiling. They even began ice-skating. He walked in the office, tossed his several layers on his hook and cubby, and made his way through the office to his cubicle.

"Hi, Osman," Sherrie smiled. "You look like you need to thaw. I will walk back an espresso to you. We can discuss the conference call; Dimitrios wants us to stand in for him."

"Sure, Sherrie," Osman said, nodding in agreement, "Do you want me to meet you in the conference room so we can view the copy better?"

"Yes, no worries. Meet me in ten minutes; it'll give you some time to warm up."

The boss was a mellow type—a bit of an eccentric genius who valued results and talent over stiffly sticking to protocol. Facebook and social media were part of, rather than problematic to, firm productivity. Being the Facebook addict that he was, Osman scanned his notifications like he did every day. "Nothing from Yannis…"

Once a week he left messages to Meimetis, who had not spoken to him since the incident in Neapolis. Both of them had found their way out of Greece and Turkey in the course of the last year. Yannis and Sia had boarded a plane to Australia a few weeks later with tickets paid for by Yannis's uncle, together with work permits.

Osman's exit was, of course, more complicated. He and Nilufer left Athens the same day Nilufer arrived, barely making the evening flight to Izmir. His father Omer had been dead for several hours, and his sister Fatme arrived that same afternoon from Ankara, cursing her brother for "bringing shame on our good name, and for sending our father early to his grave." It almost erupted into a deathbed-side brawl with other close officer friends heaping abuse on Osman until Nilufer stepped in with a voice that honored no opposition: "Cool it, now!"

Again, Osman was stunned by her nerve and inner authority, to which all showed an unexpected deference. She set to planning the funeral along military lines, and the after-funeral wake, Western style, at her home. Here, too, she and Osman accepted the condolences of neighbors, friends, Colonel Celik's military colleagues, and family, but Nilufer made sure that the tone of the event was reverential yet subdued, lacking in the drama that Mediterranean people, regardless of creed or ethnicity, seem to stir.

A Turkish general—his father's former commanding officer—stopped by later, when most of the guests had left. He offered his condolences coldly to Osman, Nilufer, and Fatme, gave chocolates to the kids, and then essentially dismissed the women "for a private talk with Osman Bey."

Nilufer melted back, proffering sweets, coffee, raki (the General was known as a declaratively secularist Turk and a hard drinker), and left them in the parlor, shooing remaining guests and family to the balcony. Though Nilufer held court in her home, with the General she fully backed down.

The General sat down opposite Osman, as Nilufer left the two with sweets, meze and Osman's stash of raki. "No Nilufer, thank you, I will pour," the General said. "I am sure the children need you." Had he said, "Dismissed," the point would hardly have been clearer.

Osman felt a drop of sweat on his chest; thankfully a breeze blew in from the Bay of Izmir. This was not going to be fun. It was a one-sided conversation:

"Osman, I don't think I need to mince words with you. You are an educated man, so I will pay you the compliment of being direct and to the point. I have always cared about your family, and of course your late father. I am not happy about what you did, but in a manner, I respect it. The man your father killed was a soldier: a brave one who stared death in the face unblinking. He did not deserve to die like that. Your father's CO was a psychopath, and in many ways your father's decency singled him out. He saved a Cypriot family, and pistol-whipped one of his own men for raping a teenage Cypriot girl. His CO made an example of him, and Omer never forgave himself."

"I know this, General Efendi—that he carried this wound," Osman said, and quickly added, "Apologies for interrupting."

The General held his hand up, signaling for him to be quiet. "Osman, it is done now. Your father came to me when you were in Greece. He was always tinkering with history, and as proud as he was to be Turkish, he knew that he had Greek ancestry. He knew you would find things out. I think he knew his days were numbered. He also knew about your wife's secret Greek ancestry..."

At this, Osman again interrupted, "What, he did? For how long?"

"For years, Osman. What did you think? We are the Turkish army; we are the republic—until recently. Your father detected Nilufer's eccentricities, and we traced her to a small clique of secret Christians. We had been monitoring them anyway—still do. They were always quiet and unobtrusive, and your father respected his daughter-in-law greatly, too much to make this an issue. He was a liberal, to use your American term, in so many ways."

"I only found out recently, while in Greece, about Nilufer," Osman offered, smiling at the thought of his father and recalling the dozens of times when, in conversations with Nilufer, an indulgent, knowing smile had crossed his face.

Now the General switched to his clipped, well-learned English: "Osman, it is time to talk about your future. Here in Turkey, you have none. If it has not happened, your employer will soon fire you. You are *persona non grata* with most of the officer corps. Though your boss may be an Erdogan boy, he is hardly going to welcome you back after embarrassing Turkey and using a business trip as a lark to find your roots. You never really belonged here, as your father used to say. He asked me to help you go to America. I am sure you knew I was behind the scenes on that. I am now offering to help get you started. I understand your father's home was to be split between you and your sister. She lives in Ankara and will no doubt want the money. Then you each have an apartment in this building. I have an investor—an ex-military colleague who has the money—who will make you a very reasonable offer to purchase the apartment building."

Here the General wrote out a sum, in euros. "Take it to a realtor." Anticipating Osman's response, he held up his hand. "I know it may not be, as the Americans say, 'top dollar,' but it is hardly unfair. It also comes with the advantage of time not being of the essence. You can look for where to go abroad and then execute the deal. The cash will help you get started." As Osman was going to interject, the General said, "Your sister, Fatme, will agree to this; I will make sure of it."

The General poured another raki, savoring the flavor. "This is good; sometimes Nilufer, the dear lady that she is, would bring some down for us when I visited Omer."

"I know, the raki generally left quicker than if I drank it alone. It was well worth it for him—and you—to have enjoyed it!"

The General stood up and shook Osman's hand. "Osman, I am not a sentimental fellow; our republic required calculating technical types, and our job is far from over..." He thought for a moment, adjusting his aviator glasses, which were expensive and squeaky clean. "...the new custodians of this country of ours will ruin it. I would not live here if I was young, and you should not, either. Go with my blessing, and know that your father loved you." The General put on his well-tailored blazer, which was also crisp, elegant, and immaculate.

With that the General was gone. Osman waited for him to leave the apartment to start crying, and then the sobs came uncontrollably. He continued to cry later on, when he found, in his father's desk, the letter his father referred to in his dying message.

My Dear Son:

I have always told you that some doors are not meant to be opened. Remember the parlor in your *dede's*[26] house that was only for weddings and funerals. Now you will have to open the parlor for me. Perhaps it is my fault: my own obsession with history and books is the one thing we really have in common.

I knew about our family's Greek roots, and how my father's grandfather came from the Mora; I did not know details. I also knew that my mother's family came from Cyprus and were Greek Cypriots who converted to Islam. I am mostly Greek in origin, and I always felt somehow that I had to prove my Turkishness. When we landed on Cyprus, I felt very badly for the Cypriots—all of them—and in one case, I beat one of my own men who had raped a Cypriot teenage girl. I brought her to the hospital myself. I got into trouble with my major—a sick fellow who knew I had Greek origins and who claimed I was soft on Greeks. He ordered me to shoot the captured Greek commandos, or he would arrange my own demise.

I am not justifying what I did. I could have refused and been shot for desertion. Your mother, and you kids, would

---

26 Turkish for "grandfather." Versions of the same word are used in Bulgarian and Serbian.

have been without anything but the most meager pension, and you would have grown up—in Turkey—as the son of a disgraced soldier. How about that?

I sold my soul to buy you the life you have today: the education, the good life, the ability to study and to learn a different way of thinking. You debate by the pen, while I had to live and die by the Sword, as the Christians' Jesus would say. I have lived with this pain all of my life, with the face of my victim before my eyes at least once a day.

I will miss you, your sister, and your lovely wife, and most of all the two divine children you and Nilufer are raising. Please do not mourn me greatly, but do honor me a little.

Baba

Osman often thought of this letter, and the encounter with the General, whenever the realities of life in Canada proved too much for him. His story carried far and wide in the Greek media, and among the readers of the incident in Greece was a Greek Canadian marketing and web entrepreneur with whom Osman had held several conversations via LinkedIn about employment opportunities in Canada.

A couple of days after his father's funeral, Osman waded through thousands of e-mails, finding plenty of supportive comments, a fair number of threats, a dismissal from his company, and a couple of e-mails from his Canadian contact, indicating that there may be a position for him at his firm. He called immediately, and within a week he was in Toronto, interviewing and finalizing both an offer and the initial steps of immigrating to Canada. Osman's perfect English and Nilufer's strong French capabilities considerably smoothed the immigration process, but the offer letter highlighting Osman's strong and unique knowledge of the Turkish market, and its importance to the local Canadian business, clinched it. Within two months, just as the children finished school, Osman and family moved to Canada.

That was nine months ago, and five months of Canadian winter wore out Osman's Mediterranean resistance. He had never driven in snow, and his daily commute stressed him, as did the bone-piercing cold. He reveled in the transparent meritocracy of his firm, but the hours were longer and he found that many of his colleagues had lives he could not even remotely understand.

There were so many single parents and same sex-couples, including his boss. Whereas in Izmir he had been a typical representative of its liberal middle class, and in his old firm he was considered far too politically and socially liberal, in his new firm he felt like a dinosaur. There were several awkward situations at work when he made offhand comments that colleagues considered offensive.

Not surprisingly, Nilufer came to the rescue. At an office party hosted in the boss's sumptuous loft, she confronted the issue of same-sex couples head on with her kids, explaining in a combination of Turkish and English that in advanced countries like Canada, people were free to marry whomever they loved. It won her kudos from Osman's colleagues and boss, and it made Nilufer a popular fixture at any company function thereafter.

She meant it. Having lived with a secret about her own identity for all of her life, she could imagine the pain that homosexuals feel when forced to hide their identities. In Turkey, many of her friends were gay, and probably the mutual burden of a secret identity had attracted her to them. The openness and transparency of Canada was jarring and sometimes cold, just like the bitter weather, but to Nilufer, it was liberating. She rapidly learned English and became involved in the kids' school activities.

She also, tentatively and discreetly, began exploring her own religious identity and found that she refused to go from one sealed identity, the Turkish, to another, the Greek. Many of the Greeks she met were as equally narrow-minded as Turks, though not Mr. Dimitrios, Osman's boss. He loved her story and respected its complexity.

She would embrace her own mosaic in a country that allowed her to do so. "I was born Turkish, supposed to be Greek, but born to be Canadian," she said in an unsteady English.

Driving home that night in the freezing rain, Osman felt like he would never adjust to Canada. He was neither fish nor fowl, either in Canada or Turkey. But he had no real choice. When he arrived home to Nilufer hunched over an interactive English-language program, and the kids alternately on their iPad or jumping on the furniture, he knew they would make the transition. He would always be between worlds: a victim of the very mosaic he unearthed. But they—all three of them—would be able to celebrate the mosaic. As he embraced Nilufer, his daughter shouted, in English, with just a lingering, lovely trace of a Turkish accent, "Family hug." He smiled sweetly, reveling in the embrace.

His eye drifted to the coffee table; on it was a card with an Australian postage stamp. Seeing this, Nilufer nodded. "Yes, it's from Yannis. A wedding invitation: he and Sia are getting married." A tear came as he held his family tight.

Made in the USA
Charleston, SC
13 November 2015